SWITCHBOARD OPERATORS

ROSEHILL: PORTRAITS FROM
A MIDLANDS CITY

SWITCHBOARD OPERATORS

CAROL LAKE

BLOOMSBURY

First published 1994

Copyright © 1994 by Carol Lake

The moral right of the author has been asserted

Bloomsbury Publishing Ltd, 2 Soho Square, London W1V 5DE

A CIP catalogue record for this book
is available from the British Library

ISBN 0 7475 17118

Typeset in Great Britain by
Hewer Text Composition Services, Edinburgh
Printed in Great Britain by
WBC Book Manufacturers Ltd

ACKNOWLEDGEMENTS

I would like to thank, firstly and mostly, Xandra Hardie, for her warm encouragement and constant helpfulness; Christine Cooke, Doreen and Peter Rudge, Shelley Mullaney, Jim Hooley, for GPO reminiscences, and Graham Wootten and the Telecom Technology Showcase for access to material on the Post Office; for helpful editorial suggestions, Mary Tomlinson and Charis Ryder; and for other various and invaluable help, Liz Calder, Suzanne Kent, Graham Hoole and Julian Atkinson.

Thankyou also to workers in this country whose labour and tax contributions have enabled me to have the time to write this book.

CONTENTS

SWITCHBOARD
OPERATORS I

The Telephone Exchange in our town was built in the 1930s, just before the War. It was set behind the town's streets at the bottom of a windy windey lane which had a medieval well at its foot, dedicated to Thomas à Becket. Facing the Exchange was the Black Prince, an old closed-down cinema, with peeled hoardings and battered armour helmet with black plume. The cinema doors were fast shut, dead leaves from many autumns blew across its steps and collected behind its grille, but I could remember being taken there as a small child by Joy, who was my mother. We had walked in deep carpet and crashed Poppets about in a box, and watched the films round and round. Usually these treats began by a visit to the Telephone Exchange, where Joy worked, to 'get something from my locker'.

We would enter the building, the trellis on the lift opened like a portcullis giving way, and we went juddering up to the secret places where Joy went each day, where existed something female and twittering.

We went up and up, as though in a tower. At the time I could never understand because the entrance was square and quite small and it seemed as though we must in some way be in the air. Actually, the high part of the building was set back from the entrance. Joy took me to the Retiring Room and parked me on a chair, and the operators looked down with smiling eyes and lipsticked smiles. They wore nylons and pearls and had wonderful voices and they smelt of powder and heaven. I was fed dunked biscuits and cooed over.

'Hellllo – what's your name?'

'Aaaaah.'

'My gosh, Joy, she's the image of you . . .'

Joy had long scratchy fingernails that nipped my hands, she wore very high-heeled shoes with little butterfly bows on them, and she was quite different from my mother at home, who did the housework and cooking and told everybody what to do. My mother frequently made mock of Joy and of her clothes, but she stood washing and ironing them, all the fiddly little bits, each individual frill, each pleat, sprays of embroidery on collars.

In the evenings a rummage in Joy's handbag found objects from the GPO – a tiny silver badge, a snap of the operators' trip to Skegness, Joy's heavy pencil with its strange black dialling top, like no other pencil you ever saw. Sometimes I opened the Golden Gift Book, and between Making Felt Pictures and Hiawatha's Wedding Feast was the page showing How It Works: the Wonder of the Telephone. My crayon followed the windings of the flex, from the dialling man all the way round the page to the smiling operator. Just like Joy and her friends at the Exchange. A real switchboard operator had pageboy hair and ear plugs and she was called Gwen – or Sheila, or June – but there were lots of Gwens, they came to the house when Joy had her twenty-first birthday party, they had circular skirts and red mouths, and they laughed all the time, and played records.

In Decembers Joy dressed a small doll, or fastened bells and bows to a skipping rope, and then we parcelled it up in hollied paper and, led by her, I carried it into the big polished Switchroom at the Exchange, to hang on the Christmas tree. This was the GPO tree, aglitter with tinsel and fruiting with parcels for orphans, put there by the switchboard operators, the postmen, telegraphists, counter assistants, engineers. Everybody put a present on the great tree.

At nine I was given an exercise-book and pen, and sent along Rosehill Street to Miss Blair. She was a supervisor at the Telephone Exchange, founder-member of a drama company, adjudicator at speech festivals, and in the evenings a teacher of Elocution and Drama. It was a fashion just then with the switchboard operators to send their small sisters and daughters and nieces to Miss Blair.

So, as a child, whatever occupation took my passing fancy – nurse, sweater-girl, cowboy's wife, singer – I expected to be a switchboard operator, and by the time I went to work at the Exchange it was part of my life from long before.

'You are here to perform a service – a public service,' said Miss Armitage firmly, when we started our training. The training lasted two months, during which time we learned the basic theory of how the boards worked, operating procedure, matters relating to our exchange in particular, and the GPO codes of all the major cities. We sat at desks among stencilled sheets of information and maps of the insides of boards, and mushroom-coloured notebooks with a crown on the covers. 'When the calling subscriber lifts the receiver the Apparatus engages a switch,' we biroed slowly in our notebooks. 'As each number is dialled, electric impulses race through to the selectors and cause them to move. The first digits in a number link to the appropriate exchange. The 4 of 47338 is really 40,000, and on dialling a movable part of the selectors makes contact with the points in the 40,000 line. The next digit – 7 – is really 7,000 . . . and finally 8, which gives the specific telephone number . . . The first selector secures the route to the junction selector. The junction selector finds a disengaged junction line . . .'

'Now can you underline the next bit, because it's very important to remember,' said Miss Armitage, frowning slightly at Elly's apple put ready on her desk for lunch. '"The impulses are created not when the dial is being moved, but when the dial is returning to its normal position under the influence of a governor in the mechanism of the dial." That is terribly important to remember, it means you mustn't dial too quickly, you must allow time for the selectors to do their work . . .'

I trained with Elly, who had an alice-band and a real retroussé nose. At first I kept looking sideways at her, because I couldn't believe it. We both had our sixteenth birthdays whilst still in training and celebrated with sticky buns and coffee, and an illicit trip to the Spotted Horse, which was the GPO pub. It was set in the block of buildings with the main town Post Office, built on the site where the post-horses were stabled in the last century. We felt very daring sipping our shandies, and went back carolling 'There was a man called Michael Faraday/He discovered electricitay/Now the night-time is as bright as day/Good old Michael Faraday, de da, de day.'

Miss Armitage took us to see the Apparatus on the ground floor, and it was eerie, the deserted aisles of selectors, whirring and tapping endlessly, as everybody in the town who picked up their telephone and dialled caused the Apparatus to rattle into play. Then she took us across the road to the main Post Office building, to visit Telegrams and the Sorting Office. As we turned the corner in the huge building, suddenly before us was a telegraph boy lying along a wooden form outside a door, fast asleep on his cap. Behind uplifted hands we giggled, and a shocked, then a vague dreamy look came into Miss Armitage's face, so you could see she was Rising Above It. There was something enchanting and fairylike about her – the sudden happening upon a dishevelled male, happily snoring, the silver buttons on his jacket undone, plainly confounded her. Then she seemed to float back down again and held a finger to her lips. 'Sssshh – don't disturb our Sleeping Beauty here,' she said gently.

We had no occasion to go to the main building,

not even when carrying out the duties of Junior.
When Joy was at the Exchange, the Junior had been
sent regularly to Telegrams on errands. One time
the naughty telegraph boys had lain in wait for the
Junior, who that week was called Betty, pounced,
put her in a mail-bag and strung it up and ran off
and left her to overcome her inhibitions and actually
yell for help.

Each morning I hung up my coat and pulled my
headset out of the locker shared with Elly,
which smelled of wood and stale buns and Mémoire
Chérie, and raced up the stone stairs to the
Switchroom. It was often Miss Armitage and
Miss Rawson who were in the vanguard to open
the windows after the – mainly male – night staff
had signed off. They scurried around in a great
flap, darting about with window-poles, and going
to drag down the huge windows at the back of the
boards. 'Uggggh! The men!' The night staff drank
and smoked and did as they liked. If Mrs Lord was
the first supervisor on duty she would examine her
fingernails and her stocking-seams, and then drawl
laconically to one of the youngest operators, 'Just
open the windows, would you, Miss Hurst.' We
signed our names at the signing desk, fastened on
our headsets, reeled our chairs round to suit our
height, sat down and took the first call – 'Number,
please?' 'Number, please?' 'Number . . .' echoed
down the boards. The working day had begun.
    The Switchroom was large and oblong, with par-
quet floor and high glass-domed roof, from whence
the daylight streamed. The noise was thick, dense,

as from a great hive – zzzzzzzzz zzzzzz zzzzzzz, neither falling nor rising. All around were set the high boards, each board face multiplied around the room fifty/sixty times, and there were over a hundred positions. At the top of the room was the Chief Supervisor's desk, covered in telephones, pens, notebooks, a bowl of flowers. At the other end was the Divisional Supervisor's desk, with its high top and Log Book, and equipment for listening-in to operators. Down the centre of the Switchroom were low boards manned by experienced operators who took calls for Directory Enquiries and Faults. On the polished wooden top of these boards stood flowers and cardboard lists of doctors' numbers and chemists' rotas. The Junior sat on the other side, ready to run if any operator buzzed, periodically collecting dockets, filing them, and taking them to Accounts.

At the very top of the ordinary boards, so high the smallest operators had to stand on the raised shelf on the bottoms of their chairs in order to reach, were the circuits used for checking that local numbers were in use. Next came the dialling circuits, in alphabetical order, and banded in different colours, the biggest sections blue for London Faraday, and green for Nottingham Trunk, over which most of our calls were routed.

Before using a circuit you first tested it rapidly with the tip of your plug, and if it was engaged it fizzed. At the bottom of the board-face were tiny glass lamps which glowed as local numbers rang the Exchange. When answered, the light went out. The corded plugs in their dull orange jackets criss-crossed over the boards in ever-changing connexions (the GPO used this spelling), the switchboard operators endlessly weaving patterns, like busy innocent Fates, not willing destiny, merely carrying it out, inserting and releasing plugs, poising their fingers and dialling with their pens, describing a circle, a circle, as the dial is pulled round, hands flying about the boards like white birds, 'I'm trying to connect you . . .' '. . . trying to connect you . . .' The weavings disintegrating and reforming, in an endless web of communication.

On the Incoming boards you became pure voice, there was so little to say. The calls came in from distant exchanges wanting access to local exchanges, or local numbers they were having difficulty dialling.

'Derby' 'Derby' 'Derby' sang out all around.

'Hello, Derby, can you help me to Belper?'

'Through to Belper.' That was it. There was nothing more to say, except 'Derby' over again to another call.

'Hello, Derby, can you help me to Mansfield?'

'Through to Mansfield SFJ.'

This was a warning – straightforward junctions were dicey connexions, you had to wait for a faint pip and then speak at once, or the connexion was lost. Often the distant operators came back several times. A tiny lamp glowed LS for Leeds. Leeds was a straightforward junction and when they rang in there was always silence on the line.

'Derby. Derby – ' click click with your peg, to try to release the circuits. 'Hello, Derby Derby Derby.' The line whistled and creaked as the Apparatus contorted. I sang out repetitively from joy, not impatience.

'Hello, Derby Derby Derby, this is Leeds Leeds Leeds,' sang back Leeds melodiously. 'Hello, Derby – ' when these are the only words you can utter you have to make them as wonderful as possible, and the voices all around made me think of birds – robins or nightingales – who sing out their all in a silken fountain of song which only says one thing, one thing, one thing, for there is nothing more or better they can say.

There were over a hundred switchboard operators at our exchange, working different rotas each week, between eight in the morning and six in the evening. We weren't allowed to work later than six – you had to be twenty-one to do that. Most of the telephonists would have married and left by then anyway, so we didn't cast much thought to it.

The switchboard operators were a tiny fraction of the GPO workforce, for at this time the Post Office was the most important single employer of labour in the country. There were over 400,000 workers, including administrators, power and electrical engineers, architects, medical officers, solicitors, typists, clerks, postmen, sorting clerks, counter officials, telegraphers, messengers, telegraph boys, PO railway workers, wireless station operators and cable ship crews.

We were not allowed to leave our positions, there was no walking about just as you fancied. Each operator followed a specific weekly duty in which times and board-positions were clearly designated.

Each day you moved position several times. Why this was so, I never knew. Perhaps it was designed to thwart boredom, or to keep the flow of air moving, to prevent cliques, or maybe to prevent mass hysteria or synchronised menstruation.

'See you in the Retiring Room at half-past, fruit.' Chris Cross would patter in, late as usual, and mouth the words at me on her way to her position. Chris had a scatty air and irrepressible high spirits, she was almost never miserable. To look at, she made me think of Cicely Barker's Willow Fairy, her eyes forming a line of amusement, and long bronzey-fair hair; with colossally high heels she gave the impression of stepping tiptoe.

Pamela Heath would wander into the Switch-room from Clerical, her cardigan limp about her arms like a cloak or cast-off wings. She was a freckled redhead who had married her boss and then got bored, so when she came to the GPO she was already married. In the past this had been unknown, and it was still fairly unusual, although sometimes operators came back after their children had grown. In the early days of the century, switchboard operators were always unmarried, and as soon as they did marry they took their dowry and left. The dowry system still operated. The GPO and the Union had had a scrap about it a few years before, and there was still an ongoing bicker about whether a married woman could be Chief Supervisor. The GPO had resisted so far. The Union had won the right for an operator, on her marriage, to choose not to take her dowry and thus to retain her position;

or to take her dowry and return to work after her marriage at the bottom of the seniority list. Both of these options were bitterly opposed by some of the unmarried supervisors.

'You see,' explained Miss Armitage in her careful dulcet tones, 'the dowry system may seem quaint to you, but it was initiated when the Telephone Company was first put under the control of the Postmaster General in 1912, and it was to provide dowries for those girls who married and a career for those who didn't marry, and it would have been *most* unfair for a girl to expect both,' she finished reprovingly.

Chris shot me an agonised look and whispered, 'It's the 1960s outside, fruit, but we're stuck in a timewarp in here.'

Miss Armitage was popularly supposed to be in love with the GPO. 'Oh, she was really rather sweet,' declared Joy, in her married way. Joy had gladly taken her dowry, tossed her flowers and pit-patted away on her high-heels with her Rescuer. As a wedding present Miss Armitage had given her a patchwork teacosy of her own devising, and on visits I sat at the breakfast table of the married pair picking out Miss Armitage's summer dresses in its hexagons. 'I love it,' said Joy, handing her husband the sugar for his cornflakes, 'because each day I can think of her in her different dresses.' She never saw Miss Armitage again, but the teacosy gave her happy thoughts.

In summer Miss Armitage wore cotton frocks stitched by herself; in winter under her tweed suit she wore pale blushing blouses and little brooches, and everything about her was delicate, and vulnerable. She had kind grey eyes, and was extraordinarily thin, with naturally curly hair, cut very short. She stressed loyalty to the GPO, and you could see she probably hadn't changed much since being a prefect at school. Outside of work she was a Hospital Visitor, it made her happy to fill baskets to take to patients; and she ran a Brownie pack.

One of the girls, whilst training at Nottingham, said eagerly, 'Once you're GPO trained, you can leave and get a job anywhere.'

The Training Supervisor replied frostily, 'That would be dishonest and extremely disloyal. The GPO has the considerable expense of training you, the least it can expect is loyalty from its staff. If you intend to do that, then you shouldn't be here.'

The Chief Supervisor was Miss Marriott, known among the girls as Dolly, or the Meringue, probably because of her extra-sugar politeness ('I'm so sorry – here's a P.18' – as she handed you a serious disciplinary charge. But it was an apocryphal story) and her white spun-sugar bouffant, which at times of great moment she decked with a black silk bow. She ran a very efficient exchange, in spite of gripings from us, the underlings.

The Ellys of Joy's time had disappeared into wives or supervisors, and so were known to us only by their surnames.

Generalising, you could put the operators into four sections – women who had never married and who had often come to resemble the popular unkind depiction of spinsters; unmarried career women, who tended to be dressy, stylish, competent people who often had married lovers, although this was never alluded to; girls who were waiting to make an advantageous marriage or girls whose engagements were long because they were saving for deposits on houses to move into when they married; girls who would leave when they married or − more often now − just before their first baby was due. The last category formed the majority of the switchboard operators.

If the Switchroom under its glass dome sounded like a vast hive, then the Retiring Room sounded like a bird colony, as girls chattered, squealed, laughed, somebody's engagement ring was handed about to be admired, cutlery and crockery came together noisily, snatches of conversation floated about: 'Ooooo, it's *lovely* . . .', 'Uggggh, this cabbage,' 'Quick − I'm on an Urgent − where's Chris?' 'She's nipped out to buy some cheekyboo clothes . . .' Teaspoons clicked against mugs, tapwater splashed into the sink, headsets were thrown over the backs of chairs, as the Vals and Susans and Pats sped in to snatch breaks, and departed again to their work.

Pinned to the green baize of the noticeboard in the corner were holiday postcards; thank-you letters for leaving presents and snaps of new babies; a Civil Defence rota; a handwritten letter on perfumed paper from the Chief Supervisor asking for volunteers to collect on Wings' Night; the times for Choir; dotted newspaper clippings, of Miss Blair standing by a french window and pointing a gun at a man, and Sal Barker addressing an open-air union meeting; a blurred photograph of early switchboard operators, their heavy headsets like yokes, bee-stung lips and coiled hair, their eyes dazzled with the voices they were hearing. And a photo of the first Retiring Room, full of Victorian shade and virginal lilies.

Apart from the social club and the youth club, there was the Union and various union committees. Linda's granny showed her how to charleston, and she started up the Charlestonettes, who danced and gave their fees to charity. Miss Marriott, impressed by the movement of Terpsichore among her switchboard operators, decreed that a payment from the GPO Welfare Fund be made for the purchase of fringed dresses and feathers. Girls collected in the Retiring Room to finger the fringes and blow the feathers, and the Meringue sailed regally in to inspect all frills. Miss Blair conducted a poetry reading group, and Joy took Keep Fit and Health and Beauty classes. Phyllis and Barbara ran the Choir, which met on Tuesdays. GPO girls had a reputation for their voices, from Kathleen Ferrier to Babbity Blue (Babbity *who*? – 'I'm such a young girl, don't make me' we sang together heartily all one summer when the record came out, before tinkling into giggles). The GPO Choir sang its way through hits from musicals, traditional songs, operettas and a little light classical, and afterwards repaired to the Spotted Horse.

On Wednesdays I went to a meeting of young socialists. We held discussions and passed resolutions, and afterwards went off to the Gainsborough to drink coffee and talk more. If the Telephone Exchange was all female, the world of politics was mainly, though not exclusively, male. Richard was the same age as me but he still went to school. Over his school uniform he wore a capacious black duffel coat, on the back of which he had painted in white gloss a huge CND symbol. He had short curly fair hair and small blue eyes, which sparkled behind spectacles if he heard an idea that interested him. As he talked, he pushed his spectacles up from time to time, and sounded earnest – even severe – but he was quite funny really.

When I was on a split shift we sometimes met up in the Gainsborough. He pushed his satchel under the dark wood table and we sat for ages with our coffee. Anything you told Richard he was interested in, whatever it was, he furrowed his brow and you could tell he was trying to fit it into a scheme of all the things that he knew so far. On the side of his satchel was penned in school ink Richard Hollister, some crossings out, then Lower Fifth, Bemrose School, Derby, England, Europe, The World, The Sun's Orbit, The Galaxy, The Universe . . . I read idly, as he sorted through his pockets to find something.

'Why did you put dots after Universe?'

'Oh, that. I wrote it in the first form,' he said dismissively.

A very few years before he had been a boy in short trousers with a stamp collection, a dog, and parents. Now he was big and tall and the head of the household, for his father had died suddenly, and together with home responsibilities, Richard was also seriously considering the best way for the world to go forward. He knew lots of people, everywhere.

'Gosh, I'm due back on the boards soon – I'll

17

have to fly.' I got up and buttoned my coat and sorted some coins out.

From the other side of the packed room Gaily Smith, another operator, called, 'Hi – wait for me. Don't let's rush, I'm a fatalist, if we're late, we're late.' This certainly had novelty as far as Exchange time-keeping went.

Richard looked up from where he was sitting, a little ruck of concentration over his eyes, and announced vigorously, 'Fate is an excuse for people to do nothing. It's important to fight against the concept of Fate, or we'll all go down the nick.'

Gaily uttered a little timorous, 'Oh,' and shot out. When we were in the street she said, 'Who was that boy?'

At the Telephone Exchange most of us, I think, without saying so, regarded Fate and Love as being synonymous. You would meet someone and fall in love and life would never be the same afterwards, even if it wasn't happy. Mostly this business involved a boy, church, and a white dress. Apart from the supervisors – and even some of them – we were all waiting. Waiting for Fate, waiting for Love.

'Marriage is stupid. I believe in Free Love.' That's what we called it at the Branch.

'What a load of old jolly tripe, fruit,' said Judy agreeably, blinking amiable little eyes at me through her freckles. I loved Judy, she had red hair and thick pink ankles, she had a St John's Ambulance certificate and if you were sick she was called from the boards to attend to you. She was the last person I ever had a schoolgirl crush on, she let me pick the hymns for her wedding service and in the mornings when I was on a nine o'clock shift I stood at the bus-stop scowling at her new husband.

We sometimes discussed men but not sex, ever, although it was present in conversations in oblique form. 'Anthea says by the time they had shifted the beds about and put everything straight they were so shattered they ended up spending the first night of their honeymoon in separate beds.'

This was met with grins and Terri looked up from her crossword over her glasses and said, 'I take everything I hear about *that* subject with a *big* pinch of salt.'

Not long after starting work I was given a Tampax after the pad dispenser in the cloak-room had broken. I bolted the door behind me and looked around at the stone floor with its white scatter of somebody's powder; the porcelain lavatory, pebbled sunshiny window and cream walls; the toilet-roll with each individual serrated sheet carrying crowns and the endless message Her Majesty's Property Her Majesty's Property Her Majesty's Pr . . . The Tampax lay in my hand like a firework that might suddenly go off. Outside the door was a line of girls spraying lacquer in front of mirrors and Janet and Rita, waiting to see if I could use the Tampax. Nothing would be said, but they would know.

'Is it alright?' enquired Janet, deceitfully solicitous.

'It's fine,' I answered coolly. They exchanged looks.

*　　*　　*

Rick and I went about the silent midnight town with paintbrushes, putting CND symbols on the Council House, the Guildhall and the town clock, the main Co-op and Florence Nightingale's skirt. Against the night sky stood the cathedral, the shops dense and black now, the roads deserted, the lighted hands on the clock with no one to see them, except us. The town was after all quite small, you couldn't see much of it at once because it had grown up straggling along a river, which now ran under the main street; the buildings were higgledy and there was no grand sweep as of a city.

'When the revolution comes,' said Rick, 'it will be very useful, having you at the Telephone Exchange.'

'Will it?' I said, pleased. I swapped the carrier-bag holding the wet paintbrushes into the other hand, then had misgivings. 'Well, I don't know,' I said. 'I don't specially want to be shot if I give somebody the wrong number. I mean, Trotsky had the drivers shot if the trains were late, that's not very fair. Diane's dad's a train driver and I don't think they'd like it very much . . .'

'No,' he said patiently, 'but we have to try to comprehend something larger than ourselves and our own experiences. These were serious men who had a destiny and a revolution to make. They had to get everything right or the whole thing would have collapsed. That's why even little things can be important. It could be vital, having you at the Exchange. We may need you to destroy all connexions with counter-revolutionary forces, or to make sure crucial contacts are maintained with

HQ. You know, we're right in the middle of the country here . . .'

'Gosh. Yes, so we are.' I was thrilled and excited, the sleepy night town seemed suddenly prickling and alive and full of possibility.

The next day found me yawning on the boards between calls, logging the start of a call, then flipping back the pegs along the board one by one, to check the subscribers were all talking.

'. . . yes but, Joan, honestly, I was so mad with her . . .'

'. . . our Mr Kimp is waiting to speak to you . . .'

'. . . should I? Why should I? You can if you like but I'm not going to . . .'

'. . . when you rang before who did you speak to?'

'. . . at five past three, arriving at two minutes past seven . . .'

'. . . in the cupboard. I'll go then, Harry . . .'

'. . . he's late every morning and he always comes without his swimming-trunks . . .'

'. . . you say one of our flues that was fitted a month ago . . .'

Disconnecting the plugs from the finished call, hastily noting its duration and the time it finished, I filled the docket and took another call. It was Refresher in the afternoon. That would be a break to attend a class on some obscure point of operating procedure, held once a week. It made a change. In the evening I was staying in, from tiredness and lack of funds. Next day was pay-day, with the arrival of the brown packet that always looked plumper than it actually turned out to be, once you'd pulled all the explanations from the pound notes. But it was good, to get a wage-packet – the money you have earned. Inspite of all the singing and the feathers, we really worked hard.

THE GIRL WITH THE GOLDEN VOICE

In the beginning, there were boy operators who staffed many of the early exchanges. They didn't last long for apparently 'the work was not found to be suitable for their venturesome temperaments'. Young females were thought to be easier to control. Discipline was strict at the Exchange, you could never move about at will, or even talk when the tiny lamps glowed. But on Saturday afternoons traffic was slack, and there was only a skeleton force on duty – ten or twelve girls, a couple of Directory operators, and a supervisor. The Saturday supervisor was a low-ranking or even an acting supervisor, who in the week reverted to being a senior switchboard operator. As calls were fewer, the atmosphere was slightly more relaxed, and the customary dense buzz had disappeared. Although a rota system was in force, so all operators took turns to follow the same duties, the married or engaged operators usually preferred to pay the younger girls, who were always short of money, to work for them. So the complement of switchboard operators on Saturday afternoons who were young and silly was greater than usual. It was the best time of the week; even Jennifer, who was our age but could always get money, started to work her own Saturday shifts.

It must have been a Saturday afternoon when Kathleen Ferrier did her hand-stands in the Switchroom: we couldn't imagine it being possible at any other time. 'Although I can just picture the bit where the supervisor says, "Miss Ferrier, where's your decorum?"' said Chris, 'because they still talk like that now.' The sweep of parquet floor, fierce-smelling with polish, was ideal for doing cartwheels.

When the sole supervisor went for her break, a frolicsome fifteen minutes ensued. Magistrates and vicars were rung up and connected to a London call-girl. Lord Ripley, a particular Exchange bugbear because of his utter rudeness – he probably regarded us as glorified forms of housemaid, infuriatingly not under his control – had his line put straight into the Waterworks. This meant he couldn't dial out, and if he picked up his receiver there was a horrid clanking bashing noise on the line. 'Can't reach the bookies for fifteen minutes – serve the nasty old bat right.' Sweets were handed about along the boards for the only time all week, and general Misrule held sway. The Howler was put on numbers that had particularly peeved us that week: Dish of the Day was connected to the Cricket Scores, and chirped brightly of crêpes Suzette or spicy beefbake at the dry male voice uttering numbers, and listening in to them was eerie – maybe the pair of them had as much contact as many another couple, each existing in their own little worlds.

'You know, I've always wondered what would happen if I put a matching pair of plugs each in one ear, and then dialled,' said Chris. 'Something extraordinary might happen. If I could find the right number to dial maybe my whole brain would be activated and I'd invent something.'

'Yes, and maybe you'd ring the wrong number and fuse everything in there,' said Mavis squashingly.

Anyway, nobody ever tried this, because the plugs could give little shocks if you were working very fast and had damp palms.

It became the custom at one period to ring the Barracks on Saturday afternoons and have a little chat with the soldiers. They were bored too on Saturdays. Of course, we couldn't give our names, or we would have been in trouble.

'I can't possibly tell you my name,' breathed Chris, her pale eyes slitting with amusement, 'because, actually, we had to sign the Official Secrets Act, you know.' A smile flitted its way along the line of operators, from lips to lips.

'Hello,' piped up Gaily. 'My friend can't tell you her name, but she's a very tall redhead' – everybody giggled at this travesty – 'and she wants to know what you're doing right now.'

'Right now I'm cleaning my tack and thinking I might get into town tonight,' said the hopeful gravelly voice on the line.

'That's funny because tonight –' started up Janet, but she didn't get far.

Fanny Fanshawe suddenly appeared, back from her break. 'Is something wrong, Miss Farquhar?'

Without waiting for an answer, Fan plugged into Janet's board and went straight into the line, 'Hello, Caller – are you having difficulty?'

To right and left girls whipped out their plugs, unable to follow the rest of the conversation. Ten minutes later – as we knew they would – the Barracks rang us, but there was no chance now of everybody being in on it.

Susan was the lucky one to pick up the call. She turned, grinning. 'There's a call for me, Miss Fanshawe.'

'You'd better take it on the telephone, then,' replied Fan and a smirking Susan left the boards. We kept turning to watch her smile, but nobody dared plug the call so we didn't know what she was saying. Fan was at the Divisional Supervisor's desk, filling in the Log Book. She was a large girl in her late twenties, with soft fair eyelashes and a silky elemental voice.

Susan came back to the boards, grinning widely. 'He kept asking me questions about Fan,' she said. 'He seemed very interested.'

We greeted this with a mix of amused astonishment. Frances Fanshawe was one of five or six senior operators; they tended to wear twinsets and shapeless skirts in the winter, and shapeless ill-fitting dresses in the summer, and no makeup. Entirely agreeable, yet our world of eye-shadow and boys and sitting in a pub with the Ronettes belting out of the jukebox was not their world. Nor did they seem to fit in with the Meringue's idea of what constituted a switchboard operator, for they were not fashionable enough. Nevertheless, in the relentlessness of time they floated to the top of the seniority list as other operators fell aside into marriage. Fan was one such girl, she moved about the Exchange unruffled and serene, with her pudding-basin haircut still like the schoolgirl from whom we were all in full high-heeled retreat.

Then: 'Actually I – er – made a date for Fan.'

'*What!*'

From the desk Fan looked up sharply, and we lowered our voices.

'Honestly, Susie-fruitie, she won't go and she'll probably give you a P.18 when she finds out.'

'It doesn't matter,' said Susan, 'she doesn't have to go. Chris can go.'

'Of all the cheek' – Chris's voice skipped lightly up the sol-fa but she didn't sound too displeased. 'Well, one of us can go – we can draw lots.'

'I must say, as it's your idea, I think you should be the one to go,' said Mavis indignantly.

'Can't can't *can't*, angels,' sang Susan. 'I'm seeing Bill tonight and I can't put him off.' Susan was as blithe as could be during the day, but apt to ring people up in the middle of the night to tell them she couldn't see much point in it all.

We drew matchsticks from a beaker, and Ann got the short one. 'Oh *no*, I don't think I can.' She laughed but sounded quite excited about it. Then she had misgivings, because she had a kind heart. 'No, but – do you think we ought to? I mean, Fanny might like to go herself.' But even as she said it, it sounded ridiculous. For a start, Fan was nearly a supervisor, and the idea of her larking about over the telephone wires with the Barracks was beyond the scope of the possible.

'Fan isn't interested in men.'

'She *must* be, underneath.'

'She won't want to meet him. She won't care,' said Rita. That was true. Fan's idea of fun was sitting at home in the evenings with her mother eating caramels and breeding dogs.

On Monday morning we were buzzing with curiosity in the Retiring Room. Ann turned up with a big grin. Not only did she have a tender heart – she also couldn't tell a lie. When she had met the soldier under the town clock she found it impossible to pretend she was Fan. 'I can't help it, I didn't feel like a Miss Fanshawe . . . So I just told him she couldn't come and had asked me to come and tell him.'

'Ann, you ninny, he'll think it's alright to ring in and ask for her now, if you said that.'

'No he won't. I told him she's only there on Saturday afternoons, and we get into trouble if we're rung in the week. Anyway, I don't think it much matters, because I'm seeing him myself on Thursday,' she finished.

'What's he like, then?'

'He's spot on, peachy.'

By sheer bad luck Fan was on Fault Telephonist that week. Elly heard Miss Mills say to Miss Marriott, 'The Barracks keep coming through on Faults.'

'Oh dear. We'd better send someone out to them.'

Then everything got very complicated. Ann was

seeing Pte Jimmy Morris, Chris was due next, then me, and Pauline was having her hair peroxided for when it was her turn.

'Well, you naughty little tinkers,' said Elsie Evans, who was only working this Saturday because her husband and son had gone away on a fishing weekend. 'I'd no idea all this went on – I've really had my eyes opened today.'

Janet was absolutely nuts over Al, the soldier who worked the switchboard. She was so crazy about him you could see it wouldn't come to anything. She even told him her name, which was a stupid thing to do.

'Well, you've made a howler there, Janet, and don't say you haven't been warned,' said Ronni. I forgot to tell you about Ronni, she was great, she was twenty-five and very sophisticated. She had dark blonde hair and a tattooed bluebird flying up her leg, put there ages ago, for a school dare. She was crazy over Mario Lanza records and on summer midnights swam naked in Blue Lake. She went to a dressmaker who made up Ronni's own designs, and they were like no other clothes you ever saw on anybody else, with low fur-trimmed necklines, or totally bare backs, or rainbow swathes of chiffon. On Sundays Ronni and Val Pepper put on big clumpy shoes and went hiking all over the countryside. Mario Lanza was very out of fashion but Ronni didn't care. She often worked on Saturday afternoons, because she was saving up to hitch-hike round Italy.

After a while – no doubt in the interest of greater confusion – if we rang when Al was busy he would connect us at random anywhere in the Barracks, so we didn't know who we were speaking to, and neither did the recipient of the call. This chance criss-cross of randomness made for novelty, and carried the interesting possibility of heartbreak.

There was a party near the Barracks and some of us went, but I can't remember much about it because I fell asleep. It was noisy and there was dancing, the room was smoky and rank with drink and youthful unchastity, and I fell asleep kissing soldiers. There must have been a pond there too because four girls were singing and they all fell in, everybody heard the splash and the screams.

Over in the corner Al was a golden boy whom everybody liked and wanted for their friend – Al the golden boy with dark-haired Janet clinging to him as they danced.

One afternoon we met up with three soldiers on our way through town between Day-Release classes. We went for a milkshake with them. There were five of us, so they were a bit surrounded. With their plump pink-and-white faces and baggy khaki, they looked like huge babies wrapped about with scratchy blankets. All the attention was on Stu, who was shortly to be sent to Aden. 'Will you love me tomorrow?' echoed up into the market-hall rafters, the orange-juice swirled non-stop in its glass drum, hot tea spurted into cups from a metal urn. From Joicies' biscuit stall a man called across, 'Have you got any change, June?' Over on the corner stall women scrabbled through piled mounds of lace edging.

Stu said, 'We'll be sent for intensive training

before we leave the country. That lasts two months. And when we get there, we'll have to kill people,' he said importantly.

'That's terrible.'

'I know it is but you have to do it. Kill or be killed. That's life.'

'What do you mean – you'll have to kill people? What people?' The irritation sounded ungrateful when they had paid for our drinks.

'I don't know. Tribesmen,' he said vaguely, pushing the straw about in his pink milkshake. 'I wanted a banana one but they hadn't got any,' he said.

Over on the record stall they changed the record and put on 'Que sera sera', and it was like going back into the past, it was one of those records that hung around for years and was still played.

'What's this supervisor like, then?' said Stu.

One particular Saturday Al was busy and was suddenly overseen, we inferred from the way he cut short a conversation, and said formally, 'Putting you through,' and he plugged us straight into – 'Officers' Mess', chipped out a no-nonsense voice.

'Hello,' trebled out Chris, used to melting hearts, 'is Phil there?'

'Phil who?' was the cool reply.

'Well, er, I don't actually know his surname . . . I thought perhaps you'd be able to help me,' finished Chris, triumphantly clueless, to no avail.

'My dear young woman, if you don't know his surname . . .'

Just then Fan arrived back from her break. She

came into the Switchroom and sniffed the air suspiciously, homing straight in on Chris. 'What is it, Miss Cross?'

'Nothing, Miss Fanshawe.' Fan was preparing to plug in. 'It's the Barracks, they . . .'

Fan went straight into the line. 'Hello – this is the Supervisor. What difficulty are you having?'

The dumbfounded man said, 'Well . . .' and Fan, frosty and silky, said, 'Did you call the Telephone Exchange?'

'I . . . I don't think so,' said the officer, mild and almost amiable now.

'Then why –' Fan, casting her eyes along the boards, leaned forward and snatched Jennifer's plug from the call, and backward to snatch out my plug, so I heard no more.

That evening Al reported to Janet, and come Monday morning Janet reported to us, that the man in the Mess was Al's commanding officer, and he had expressed considerable interest in Fan. Al apparently was fairly furious, because he foresaw trouble for himself.

'He's blaming me,' whimpered Janet pathetically.

'You haven't told him anything about Fan?' said Ronni warningly.

'No I haven't, I'm not *mad*, am I? Everybody would get into the most awfullest trouble, the Meringue will be tossing P.18s at us like confetti . . .'

'Miss Cross and Miss Sands, can you go for your breaks now,' said Mrs Royle the following Saturday afternoon. We unplugged and skittled off down the back stairs. On Saturday afternoons the place was deserted, chairs upside down on the Canteen tables, the Retiring Room bare and tidy, its tables polished, the big glass ashtrays clean. The lockers were closed and still, on the lockertops an arrangement of shoes, the Charlestonettes' wind-up gramophone on Linda's lockertop, a rucksack on Ronni's, a megaphone on Sal's. The Choir was practising that afternoon in the Refresher Room, in preparation for their Summer Concert that evening. Phyllis and Barbara had been bickering together about what they should sing. Barbara wanted selections from *Carmen* but Phyllis thought this was a daft idea. 'All that passion, fruitie – everybody's bound to get bored.'

'No they won't, it's very popular . . .'

'Well, we can hardly all stand there in mantillas clicking castanets, we're a choir, remember,' said Phyllis, curiously irritated. 'I don't think it's our cup of tea at all, fruit.'

Phyllis had won the day, and they had decided on the hits of Perry Como and a medley of English traditional songs, and as we passed they were into 'Magic Moments', sung as a round.

'Can you hear our little Janet caterwauling among them?' said Chris rudely.

Later, when we were back on the boards, Al rang through for Janet and Chris picked up the call. Apparently he was annoyed that Janet was singing that evening and not meeting up with him. The other soldiers all said that she was messing him about. And they wanted to know more about Miss Fanshawe. Chocolate limes came tumbling down the boards from Ann. It was warm that day and when she went for her break Mrs Royle had left the glass doors open, so we got a breeze. From the floor below the Choir's voices floated in. 'Early one moorning . . .'

'Where does Miss Fanshawe go at nights? What does she look like?'

'She's not married,' I volunteered, through my chocolate lime.

'And she's not engaged, either,' added Elly.

'But she has quite a few boyfriends,' put in Jennifer, snapping her peg back so Al couldn't hear her say, 'We don't want them to think she isn't fascinating, do we, fruits?'

The breeze from the open doors lifted hair and ruffled dockets, and carried in the voices of the Choir.

'What's her name?' persisted one of the soldiers.

'We're not allowed to tell our names to subscribers.'

'We already know it's Miss Fanshawe . . . What's her Christian name?'

Mrs Royle blew back with the next gust of wind. 'Now then – come along, my little peach-blossoms, take some of these calls,' she said, in her sharp, soft way.

A six o'clock Saturday shift was the worst one you could get. There was a gloom about the Exchange on a summer Saturday. Everyone else had had a day of ease and merriment, earlier shifts had long since departed, and there was no chance of leaving even five minutes early because there was no one

36

else to take the calls until the night staff signed on promptly at six. The building stood silent in the sunshine, and nobody waited outside.

After the concert Al and Janet had a noisy quarrel and now they weren't speaking to one another. She fell out with several of us at the same time. She was so paranoid about Al, so desperate for him, that anything that made difficulty with him made her furious. Like one of her friends standing up his brother. 'Ged waited for you for an hour under the clock, and you didn't turn up,' Janet accused unpleasantly.

'Oh well, if he can only wait a mere hour . . .' Chris broke into peals, just as under normal circumstances Janet herself would have done, but she scowled now and flounced out of the Retiring Room.

Lame attempts by her friends to patch up the quarrel led nowhere.

'Can I speak to Pte Alan Mellor, please?'

'Who's calling him?'

'Janet Farquhar.'

'Sorry, he's on gun practice.' Al had been taken off the switchboard.

After that, it got complicated. In fact, it got too complicated for me, because I always get things like this mixed up. Saturday rolled round again. Mercia, our Acting Supervisor, was at the other end of the Switchroom, and I was sitting next to Gaily Smith as she took a call. 'Number, please. One moment' – she slammed her peg back in a panic. 'Oh gosh, it's a man asking for Miss Fanshawe.'

'Well, ask him who he is.'

'Hello – who's calling Miss Fanshawe, please? Thank you. Hold the line. It's a Captain Manners, from the Barracks.'

'Oh gosh' – the operators told one another this all the way along the line.

Ann said, 'Just tell him she isn't here.'

Another operator said, 'I'll take the call.'

'Don't be silly, fruitie, have you gone loco . . .'

'Hello, Miss Fanshawe speaking.'

'Oh hello. This is Captain Manners, from the Barracks. I thought I'd better ring and let you know that I have found the person responsible and reprimanded him, and I don't think there will be any repeat of the incident.'

'Oh. Right,' said Rita, and waited.

'If there is, do you think you could possibly let me know, so I can deal with it personally before it goes too far.'

'Yes, of course. It mustn't be allowed to go too far,' agreed Rita, in an attempt at Fanny's tones.

'Then I'll give you my extension number, so you can get straight through to me.'

'Thank you.'

'Well then, that about wraps it up . . . It must be fascinating, watching all the calls come in . . .'

Rita rolled her eyes up at us, then laughed nervously back at him.

'Of course, I don't get into town much – I don't know Derby terribly well – so I don't know my way around, I'm afraid . . . is the Telephone Exchange very central?'

Rita answered his questions briefly and non-committally, but Susan came into the line and said, 'Why don't you come and see?'

Mavis sat with a hand over her eyes, as if in agony, as he agreed to a meeting.

We discussed the possibilities, and who should go. Ann thought it should be Chris, I felt Ronni was the only possible choice but, although she was amused, she wasn't very helpful. 'No, my little ones, you're on your own with this one. If you're so keen, Sylvia, why don't you go yourself?'

'Heavens no, don't send Dormouse, she'll fall asleep,' said Ann, and it was true, I did keep falling asleep.

'Well, you're not roping me in – I don't sound anything like Fanny,' said Ronni firmly, and she didn't – she had a little growl in her voice.

As soon as she got to hear about it, Janet wanted to go, partly to spite Al. Every single person thought this was a stupid idea but there were no other volunteers. Once she had decided upon going, she had misgivings. 'Whatever shall I talk about?'

'Well, Fanny would probably sit telling him about Brandy's puppies, and when it would be best to worm them.'

'I think that would be quite interesting,' I said.

Chris said, 'Yes, fruit, it might be *quite* interesting but it wouldn't be *very* interesting, especially if you're with a captain in the Army.'

'Well, what are you supposed to say then? – "Do tell me how you load your rifle?" – that wouldn't be as interesting as puppies.'

'I shall wear my tapestry dress,' said Janet. There

was a big fad for tapestry dresses, and the way we wore them, they didn't look medieval, they were tight and sleeveless and cut in one piece, and as you walked they rode up. I hankered after one for ages, and you couldn't borrow one because they were so tight they acquired the owner's shape.

Then, uncertainly, 'Do you think that would look okay?'

'Not too bad, fruitie,' said Ronni, stubbing out her cigarette and reaching for her headset, 'but put an iron over it first.'

Whilst consternation whizzed between our ranks, Fanny was glimpsed serenely tucking into a chocolate bar. She seemed to move about in a dream, adrift yet not apparently unhappy. There appeared to be no element of anguish in her life, as far as you could tell; she went about the Exchange, big and soft and dreamy, although inside the hormones must have been rioting like cherubs for her to have such a complexion.

We all gathered in the Retiring Room on Monday morning to hear how Janet had got on. She shrugged her shoulders and said, 'It was obvious I didn't sound like Fan, so I just said she couldn't come. He was okay about it, he took me for a meal. He asked some questions about Miss Fanshawe – what was she like, was she strict – all that sort of thing. So I had to sing for my supper! Yummy meal, anyway. Well, I was eating this scrumptious coffee and chocolate pud, and felt I had to say something, so I just told him a few things. Of course, I made them all up . . .'

When I asked what he was like, Janet gave

me a hopeless little look, because she was still stuck on Al.

'No, come on, cough up, fruit – what is he like?' urged Mavis.

'He's alright, he's called Ian Manners, and he must be in his *thirties* – it was like being taken out by your granddad.'

The Barracks rang through to say they were sending two soldiers, Mike and Stu, before he left for good, because they wanted to see what Miss Fanshawe looked like. Could she come down, or look through a window? We asked Pamela, who had recently gone platinum blonde, to come and wave out of a stairs side-window. 'What are they up to now?' she asked Ronni, but Ronni just laughed. At five past five a cageful of switchboard operators went down in the lift. Outside with the other men waited the soldiers, Mike and Stu waiting to be bamboozled, trying to pick out which one of the crowds of girls was Miss Fanshawe.

Being seen with this Captain Manners made another lot of trouble for Janet with Al, but he and his friends seemed intrigued as well. Whoever knew what went on in their minds? He rang up, he wanted to see her, to row about it. Instead of finishing almost as soon as it had begun, their affair lasted a year, and I guess she would rather that, than it never happened at all, even though it was like treading on knives for her, and then he left her.

We began to feel we had created a monster who wouldn't leave us alone, and we didn't know what to do with her. 'Miss Fanshawe's left,' said Gillian discouragingly, but the Barracks didn't believe it.

The situation changed suddenly without resolution. Fanny disappeared for six months into Clerical, never to go near the Switchroom in all that time. Al was no longer on the Barracks switchboard. We found other things to do on Saturday afternoons, other people to ring . . .

Fan had been a switchboard operator ever since leaving school, and she didn't appear to have a social life outside work. After a while you can become used to being just a voice, tickling the air-waves, calling forth other voices, crying out that you exist by the utterance of a single word. When I was doing the Junior duty, I looked over the boards at Fanny's face as she took Directory calls, and I realised. She knew exactly what she was doing. Maybe she only knew while she was speaking, and she blanked it out afterwards. In an essential way she existed then as she existed at no other time, her body burnt away into her own true essence. Whilst in Training, I remembered one of the Training Supervisors had grabbed me firmly round the wrist and said, 'Yes. You are doing it correctly but you are not giving your *all*.' She banged my wrist up and down as she spoke. My all?

'Of course – speak out – this isn't just a job, this is a *service*, you must *give* of yourself, commit yourself . . .'

Maybe that was what Fan did. She gave her all. Perhaps there was no other time or place when her all was needed. Her face as she took calls was slightly smiling, a tender smile for all the people she spoke to and would never meet, and she was floating, floating – a voice waiting for a body.

LESSONS

The cathedral clock was chiming nine down St Mary's Gate as, one by one, we hurried into college, past the bikes padlocked to railings and the motorbikes heaped up against the buttresses at the side of the building. Swinging baskets of books and flasks of tea, everyone scurried down the narrow corridors of the old County Offices building. At this time the Technical College was expanding but had no new building, and was starting up annexes all over town wherever it could get a toehold.

Until the age of eighteen, all GPO switchboard operators had to attend the Tech for one full day a week, during term-time, in preparation for the Civil Service Exam (lowest grade). Attendance was also in keeping with the general feeling that education was necessary for everybody. Theoretically, if you didn't pass the exam, you had to leave. 'Angela didn't pass and she wasn't chucked out,' was a soothing verbal tablet regularly handed about to induce calm.

In the morning Mr Christian took us for English, History, and Civics. He wore waistcoated silver-grey suits and told us about Aristotle and the Just Society, about Derbyshire customs, and about the Industrial Revolution. He invited our opinions on these matters, and altogether his lessons were civilised and civilising experiences, conducted with ease and charm.

Although I say it myself, we behaved like lambs for Mr Christian. All our pent-up adolescent blood-lust was reserved for Mr Cox.

'Now *don't* start off the afternoon talking, or stick your legs out from under the desks,' Kath had advised when I first started, 'because he's usually been to the pub at dinnertime and if he comes back in a temper and his nerves are bad, he'll kick you,' she said alarmingly.

Kath Jennings was immensely popular. Eventually she got a transfer to a London exchange, but was still famous among us for her good nature and her long eyelashes.

'Not as long as Kath's.'

'Not bad – Kath's were longer.'

'Hold still, fruit – yes, coming along, not as long as Kath's yet.'

'Another quarter of an inch to go, Susie' – as they dipped into a pot of Magic Eyelash Grower and measured each other's lashes with a ruler.

'My mother says Vaseline is just as good as that stuff and a damn sight cheaper.'

'I wonder what Kath used?'

'Kath didn't use anything – her eyelashes were always like that.'

It was true about the kicking. Mr Cox would come

in, the door slamming behind him, cast glares about the class from under scowling neanderthal brows, and if any errant high-heeled legs protruded from under the front row of desks, he would take flying kicks at them. The switchboard operators sat on the front row – eight of us – and a classroom of empty desks lay between us and the boys, who sat on the back row. They were GPO telegraph boys, who were awaiting the magic touch of their twenty-first birthdays to turn into postmen. There was Ron, who was clever and taking his HNC, after which he would probably leave and get a different job. Noddy – named by Kath because of a supposed resemblance to the Blyton elf. Bob Greenhough, who was always grinning, and Robert Johnson-from-Sainsbury's. He was always called this, and why he was pushed in with us no one seemed to know – the college probably didn't have anywhere else to put him.

Mr Cox took us for Geography and Maths. 'Maths – huh, that's a joke. I think they mean Sums,' he said.

'Jennifer Ann doesn't like doing this,' announced Jennifer, to no one in particular.

Mr Cox's expression became more concentrated than usual. 'We all have to do things we don't like, Miss Babington.'

'Well anyway, my Billy's going to show me how to do all these nasty fractions, so I shan't be frightened of you any more,' said Jennifer, who wasn't the slightest mite frightened of Mr Cox.

'I haven't bothered with the little dot – does it matter?'

He rewarded us with a roar of fury. 'The little dot is a decimal point, of course it matters where you put it – '

'We shouldn't be having Maths in the afternoon anyway – it's a contradiction in terms.'

'Quite. Perhaps you would like to write to the governors of this establishment and tell them of your unease at the situation. In the meantime . . . Oh, get out, *you*, if you're going to be sick. I don't know why I don't just get a job in an infants' school.'

A gagging Greenhough left the room hastily amid giggles and slow handclaps from the girls.

We had Geography for an hour, and as Mr Cox had been a mining engineer about half of all lessons were about coal-seam formation in the Ruhr. That was just what we were interested in. In the next seat Val sat, politely glassy-eyed, Janet read a letter under the desk, I biroed in the stags' antlers and tail – the two beasts on the Derby coat of arms adorning the exercise-books. Somebody had chipped out with a pen-knife on the desk ANITA Anita Anita is my Wife. I looked at this, wondering about the spirit that moved behind it. Was it a chant? Somebody was in love with his wife? A pencil message announced GOD IS DEAD, to which had been added: I am obliged to inform you that God is eternal. A further scrawling addendum read: and plays left half for Derby County.

'Miss Sands – you are with us?' I smiled and waited for him to carry on with his blackboard chalking.

On occasion he went into astonishing tantrums.

He sent Gaily Smith back to the GPO for giggling. She went shopping and then went home, and nothing more was said, so Mr Cox must have softened by the following week. The most furious he was ever seen was after the end-of-year exams. He came snarling and scowling into the classroom, flapping the exam papers and histrionically casting them into the waste-paper bin.

He glared about the room. 'These are the worst results I've ever seen. You have excelled yourselves. Booby-prizes all round. These papers are an absolute disgrace. Somebody even wrote the Bay of California into the middle of America.' Nobody dared laugh, such was the danger of the situation. He went on for a bit longer. If he went too far over the top he ran the risk of getting the Waterworks on his telephone all Saturday afternoon.

'And now,' he announced, giving out sheets of paper, '*you* are going to do that test all over again. *I* shall dictate the answers. *You* will write them down. Is that clear? And I'm going to prove to the rest of the staffroom that you lot can't even *copy* the answers correctly.'

Seeing her waiting outside in the rain for a bus, he gave a lift to Val, who had red hair and scarlet lipstick and a practised confident manner with males. 'Thank you very much, Mr Cox. It was very kind of you.'

'Oh, call me John.'

'Mr Cox to me,' said Val firmly, slamming the car door and waving goodbye.

Sarcasm and rudeness were his constant method. 'Ah – Miss Cross and Miss Sands. Good afternoon, ladies. Are you sure you can spare us the time? Perhaps you couldn't get here for two o'clock because you couldn't move fast enough – you look as though you've been poured into those dresses.'

We turned haughty at this remark, exchanged looks and flapped lashes, and moved with our baskets to the empty seats.

'We were helping an old lady cross the road,' said Chris sweetly.

'Huh. I should think she needed to help you if you were wearing those shoes,' he said, furiously rude.

His lessons continued in a turgid mix of fury and cajolery. 'Oh dear. Every year it's the same. I have to roll up my sleeves and set to. The GPO issues me with a fresh batch of feeding bottles and dummies and a pile of new nappies and rattles, and then I get you lot, and I have to try and do something with you, put something into those empty little noddles . . .'

The owners of the empty little noddles watched impassively, behind eyes barred and gated with mascara, to see what was coming next.

'Now, I want my Jennifer and my Valerie and my Sylvia to listen carefully and to do well,' he said coaxingly. He ignored the boys, apart from Ron whom he did on occasion address directly, as one human being to another – a great novelty to witness.

During the two-hour break Chris and Janet sometimes went mid-day dancing at the Locarno. If you could afford it, you went to a café in Friargate, which had a thumping juke-box and steam and the constant sound of hot water fizzing into cups from a shiny metal tank. That's where the telegraph boys went. But usually, if you wanted to do anything you had to borrow money because it was the last day before pay-day and most people were broke.

'Can you lend me a shilling, just for today, fruit?'

'I was going to ask you.'

'Come on, I'm going to try to get a refund on my stiletto. It broke.'

But the man in the shoe shop only offered to replace the heel, not refund the money. We bickered at him a bit, but it was no good. We ended up going through all pockets and buying one cup of tea, price 3d, from a refreshment booth, and sharing it with straws.

There was an outpost of the college at the old Plaza ballroom, and this is where we went for our final lesson of the day, which was Plastics. The boys took off on their motorbikes, whilst we took a leisurely stroll through town, larking around and window-shopping.

There were sudden periodic crackdowns on all laxness at the Tech. A few years before, the directors of Rolls-Royce had arrived one sunny afternoon at the golf course, to find some of their apprentices, who should have been at Tech on Day-Release, in the middle of a game of golf. There was an almighty fuss about it, the directors demanding to know what their apprentices were doing at the golf course in works' time. When the general public and in particular the shareholders got to hear of the incident, they wanted to know what the directors were doing at the golf course in works' time. This maddened the directors even more, and the upshot was a general tightening of discipline. Registers had to be handed in at once, and someone was appointed to go from class to class collecting them. Suddenly, members of staff would be looking at their watches with irritating frequency.

'It's awful, it's like purdah, we can't *move*,' wailed the switchboard operators, meaning they were being timed crossing town to lessons.

Ann was rather put out because she was nuts on Mick Luscombe for a long time, and he was in the other class, with Alfie Woodhouse and Jim and Susan and Elly and the others.

'You mean,' said Janet unbelievingly, 'that *that*' – pointing at Mick Luscombe and Jim striding along the corridors in their black legshields and big leather gauntlets – 'is going to turn into . . .' We followed her eyes, to the Canteen where the Post were inoffensively tucking into their breakfasts.

Boys entered the GPO at fifteen, at sixteen they became telegraph boys and zoomed about the town on their big BSA Bantams – the envy of many a lad caught in office or factory. A telegram would come tapping in . . . he would fasten on his leathers and hurry out to where the bikes were left heaped up one on another under St James's Street archway. Soon he was away, going as fast as he liked; in the service of the GPO speed was justified. The bike was left revving at the kerb like a champing beast, the telegram handed in – 'Any reply?' – at a negative headshake he was back on his bike and had roared away before the recipient of the telegram had even made to close the door. They knew, all over the town's roads, the most dangerous stretches for accidents – outside the Saracen's Head was the worst, where a bit of metal in the road made it a particularly nasty spot – and the best places to go to make sparks. Jim's favourite place for this was the top of Oaklands Avenue. They all liked to do it in front of bus-queues or girls, they would drop down on their legshields and make a blaze of sparks and everybody would say 'Ooooooo-er-look at that!' When they got back, tiny Miss Bridgeway, who was in charge of them, would come hurrying out. 'Now then, boys, you're late – where've you been?' The big boys would look down at her with tolerant grins and say, 'Coming.'

After the age of eighteen they finished college and started foot patrol, becoming full postmen at twenty-one. Bereft of his motorbike, many a lad left, unable to face the transmogrification from black leather hell-hound into postman – surely one of the most pleasing of beings?

Fiddle Middleton was in the other class too. He bombed into work every day on his motorbike from Belper. It is not in the nature of the Derbyshire male to be intimidated by authority and Fiddle – named so by the other telegraph boys after he grew a beard, because of a supposed likeness to President Castro and a habit of starting many of his sentences with 'Fidel says . . .' – had his own opinions on most subjects. In fact, he had his own political party, and not many people can say that. This was the Belper Workers' Party. It was anarcho-syndicalist, as I recall. Now and again it even had its own duplicated news-sheet, typed very densely in capital letters. The membership of the Belper Workers' Party was sometimes as high as four and never less than one.

Although factional politically, Fiddle was an agreeable soul, and would join forces on wider issues. He professed to detest the Labour Party, yet he often stayed over in town after his shift and came to Young Socialist meetings. He certainly always turned up at big demos and at local CND meetings. On his days off he disappeared into the maw of London coffee-bars and ransacked them for new ideas – the Partisan was a particular favourite, and on his annual leave he took off on his motorbike to the Continent, to establish fraternal relations with other workers' groups.

When not at work, he could be contacted by ringing the Dog & Bear, and if he wasn't there they would go and fetch him, or take a message. If you want to know about his appearance, take a look at the blond, bearded men in Walter Crane's drawings – planters and artisans: self-sufficient, straightforward, honest men, who thought it their business to concern themselves with the state of the world.

In class discussions, Val and I were usually on opposing sides, because she supported Tory mis-rule. In spite of this, I always liked old Val and got on with her. She was a keen supporter of the Union, the UPW – the Union of Post Office Workers.

There was always a fantastically high attendance

for meetings – never less than forty girls, and usually far more, turned up, and the Canteen was packed by half-past six. It was quite usual for girls to hang around in the building for two and a half hours if their shift finished at four o'clock, in order to attend. We all believed in the Union. Unions are what you make them, they are not against democracy, they are an essential part of it. Val was a Tory, but she believed this too.

We sat in small groups at the Canteen tables, while Sal Barker, our union rep, and her deputy Pamela Heath, conducted the meeting.

Although part of the same branch, we were in a separate section from the postmen, and held our own meetings. We voted separately, but joined together with them for big meetings, marches, and demonstrations. The girls clubbed together one Christmas and gave Sal a megaphone, which she kept on top of her locker, waiting.

'Come on, Sal – when are you going to use the megaphone?'

'The day will come, don't worry,' Sal answered.

We were dying for her to use it, to call 'Everybody Out' like Miriam Karlin in *The Rag Trade*, and she did do that once in the Retiring Room, for a joke, and everybody clapped and cheered.

'Now, girls,' said Sal, 'what I'm going to do is this: I'm going to keep a spare place on the Whitley Council, and I shall rotate you youngsters, put a different one of you on each time. That way, you'll get a feel for it, you'll be able to see what goes on in negotiations, and it will be a useful lesson for you.'

Whitley was held every two months. It was very impressive, a large committee sat around a dark wood table. The Head Postmaster was there, and Mr Roland, our Branch Secretary, as well as Sal and lots of other people, I didn't know who they all were. They discussed and argued very politely about working practices and proposed new schedules. I can't remember what was said. The two who did most of the talking were Mr Roland and the Head Postmaster. They kept smiling at one another, like card-players over a hand. 'I can *ask* my members,' said Mr Roland in an amused tone, 'but I don't hold out any hope that that suggestion will appeal to them.'

After the meeting I rushed to the door to sell *Young Guard* before everybody left. Afterwards in the Spotted Horse we met up with Fiddle, who was selling *The Worker* – a little composition of his own.

Mr Roland had given me a booklet as soon as I joined, called 'Workers' Participation in the GPO'. 'What about workers' control? That's a better idea.'

'Yes. But we have to be realistic, and at the moment it's our belief that this is what suits us within the present structure of the GPO. If workers' participation is implemented properly, there'll be no problem about what it's called. We view it as a logical extension of democracy . . .'

On Wednesdays the Young Socialists met at Labour Party Headquarters. By this time the Branch had shrunk to about six members. We met informally in an upstairs room, sitting on motheaten old easy-chairs. We had grown very democratic, nobody was anxious to hold any position, so there were no formal officers because nobody wanted to be bothered. The heady early days of 25 to 30 members, the electing of officers and the calling one another Comrade Chairman and Madam Secretary had passed. There wasn't even a treasurer – the last one had absconded with the funds a year before, and nobody liked to complain officially or to pursue their recovery, because the errant treasurer had had to marry a girl and they now had a baby and they could barely manage on his wages.

Graham and Edna sometimes called in. They were engaged and had been members since the year dot – well, since 1960, which was when the calendar began as far as we were concerned. Before that, the Labour Party had had youth sections and Graham had been a teddy-boy. He still wore teddy-shaped suits with big shoulders, he had curled hair ending in a d.a. at the back, and when he went dancing he wore a shoelace tie. He worked at Royces. Edna and I had gone to the same school – she was a monitor. As each term ended and another batch of girls left, the ones who were good at Art got a job at the china factory, next door to the school. That's where Edna worked, painting Crown Derby china. 'It makes me sick,' she said, forming her mouth into a tiny petulant rosebud, 'the way people look at you when you say you work in a factory.' Can you believe this – she painted Crown Derby china, and that's what she thought about it?

The days when the Branch had socials had

passed, but Graham and Edna, who were champion rock 'n' rollers, sometimes came along to meetings and brought free tickets for Royces dances. When we arrived it was dark and the small dance floor was surrounded by tables. Graham and Edna sat sipping their drinks. They sportingly let other dancers whirl about for a while before taking to the floor themselves, and when they did so the other couples slowed down and parted like the Red Sea giving way before the Chosen, until the whole body of dancers stood about the sides of the dance floor, amazed.

David Kent had been around since the beginning too, he was in the Co-op union USDAW, and seemed to relish a reputation as a careerist. Although careerists were not well spoken of in these circles, David didn't seem to mind. In any case, he hadn't actually got anywhere yet in the power-structure, and his reputation was founded on the fact that he had once been seen at a summer-school wearing a paisley silk dressing-gown.

The Branch always had students waiting to go to university or teacher training colleges. Rick Hollister had joined, via CND, when he was in the Lower Fifth at school, and he came regularly to meetings. Rick, good-hearted and sociable, offered to hold classes on Saturdays and he gave lessons if you wanted him to, on any subject.

'This is better than the old Tech. We only learn about rotten coal-seam formation there,' I complained.

Rick, blinking a little behind his glasses in disbelief, said, 'But coal-seam formation is interesting.'

Fiddle came to take classes on the Cuban Revolutionary war, he pinned a map to the wall and pointed with a stick to the points of struggle, and we followed the moving stick across the mountains of the Sierra Maestra. 'As Che says – the Cuban Revolution is more than the instrument of one nation. It is the hope of unredeemed America . . .' said Fiddle.

Nominally, I was Minutes' Secretary, which was a post I had used to covet. At first I relished writing up long reports of Branch meetings, and did it faithfully each week, but the novelty had worn off.

The Labour Party apparatus had obviously been far happier with the old youth sections, which didn't meet up with one another and so were easier to control. They had lavished money and attention on a new national youth organisation. The local party had given the Branch a grant, and there had been little card programmes of activities, and an official YS newspaper – *New Advance* – paid for by the Party. *New Advance* was much scorned by the membership, many of whom started up their own papers. Our Branch threw out the official YS paper, and passed our own resolutions, many condemning the adult party, particularly with relation to the nuclear deterrent.

Now we had nothing, except the use once a week of a room in the Labour Party HQ, free of charge. It was actually much better: we didn't have money, just a situation and an impetus. By this time the adult party left us alone, just periodically made growling noises from a distance.

Rick took a class on the Athenians. 'They liked simple things. Their economy was simple, they had a good climate so there was plenty of food and they had leisure to pursue ideas . . .'

We listened respectfully, except for Fiddle, who said the Greeks had slavery and a contempt for work. 'You're just swallowing all the stuff put out by the British upper class, they've always fallen for the Greeks, I think they were a bunch of poncey old things in togas . . .'

'What sort of critique is that, comrade? And the Greeks didn't wear togas,' said Rick, mightily put out. 'No society is perfect, and Athens in 500BC was spectacular . . . And whatever you think, they didn't have the gold fetish that our society has, their economy wasn't held to ransom by the idea that they had to have a certain amount of a given metal before they could do anything.'

'No. That's true,' nodded Fiddle.

'Well, they sound very interesting,' said Graham, polite and loyal. 'But did they have rock 'n' roll?'

'They had choral dancing, I suppose. But I don't think that's quite the same.'

'No, I don't think it is,' said Graham, with a little smile.

Rick told us about the Socratic method, which affects the teacher as well as the pupil, it isn't just a one-way dispensing of information.

'You see, there's a process called the Elenchus, which works in five stages. You begin with strongly held opinion, which turns – as the Elenchus works – into unease. At stage three the subject suffers anguish and loss, then – confusion. This leads to the fifth stage – the desire to find out. So the process of knowledge means you start from strong belief and move to a much more creative and fluid state. With the Elenchus, to be lost is to be found. And we can all use this process in our lives.'

We left the deserted building, splitting up and going our different ways. 'Come on,' said Rick, 'I'll take you to a Communist Party meeting.' This sounded exciting, and we headed for the night-time Tech, where empty classrooms were leased out by the hour. When we got there, it wasn't very exciting, it was like a meeting of the Silver Lining Club.

'They're getting on a bit now and they don't really do too much, but they like to be kept in touch with what's going on and they're nice old things,' said Rick, shuffling through his duffel-coat pockets to fish out CND stickers. He handed me some, and we fly-posted as we walked from the meeting. 'There's no use pretending. Britain isn't a proper democracy yet, but it still could be' – his words floated hopefully into the evening. 'Of course, the real aim of education is virtue,' said Rick, grinning but meaning it.

'Oh. Yes.'

'It's not . . . *that* virtue.'

'No. It's the other one,' I agreed helplessly, trying to keep my end up, and hoping time would reveal more.

'*Virtus* isn't the narrow-minded petty virtue that we know it as, it meant something positive . . .'

The word *Virtus* was thrown about town any-way, under stags it appeared on school exercise-books, council letters, pub signs, and the dark-green corporation trolley-buses trundled dustily about town with it stamped on their sides.

Rick and I had a fad for eating food which the Athenians ate – chicken, lamb, mint, olive oil, honey – even dull old porridge acquired a glamour.

'The Athenians ate porridge,' I said at the breakfast table.

'Well. Fancy. If you don't hurry up with it you'll be late for work,' said my mother.

It was strange to see the same classrooms in the day, during Day-Release classes.

We sat waiting in the afternoon for Mr Cox to turn up, the catch of expectation in the air. He came in, letting the door slam behind him.

'Right. Get out your books . . . what is it?'

The expectation almost echoed about in the room. 'We had a meeting during the dinner hour, and it was passed by democratic vote that we shouldn't do Maths in the afternoons.'

He put his book down and came over and beamed at us.

'I'm very impressed. Well done. Full marks all round for Democracy. However, I take my instructions from Derby Education Committee, who pay my wages, and not from you lot. Nice try, gang.'

'Look, we're only thinking of the ultimate good, we don't want the Education Committee to waste rate-payers' money, and in the afternoons our brains can't take it.'

'Yes, I agree there's a problem there, but it has more to do with your having spent the entire lunch hour in the Spotted Horse, that's why your brains are dysfunctioning in the afternoons.'

'That's defamation, that is, we don't have the money on Thursdays to go to the Spotted Horse, unlike *some* people who get paid by the rate-payers and then waste the money on drink – '

'Anyway, we're fed up with you shoving useless information at us like pellets – '

'Yes, that's right, we're not your weaners.'

This analogy seemed to bring him a certain amount of pleasure, he let forth a delighted roar. 'Aaaaaah, but you *are* my weaners, Miss Babington, I'm here to pull your little tails and make you squeal, and until the Big Chop comes – the Big Chop when the GPO holds its Civil Service exam – and let's make no mistake, that will be the Big Chop as far as you lot are concerned – when you'll all be strung up and turned into sausages.' He rubbed his hands together gleefully.

Just for that, next Valentine's Day Jennifer sent him a valentine with a piglet on it.

But the feud went on.

'Now,' said Mr Cox coming breezily into the classroom. 'Before we begin, let me make it quite plain that if I get the Waterworks on my telephone next Saturday afternoon, I shall keep you all in the following Thursday. And if I get the Waterworks yet again, I shall keep you in the Thursday after that. So let's not get into this Jacobean cycle of revenge, let's all at least *try* to behave like adults.' Then he seemed to try a new tack. 'I'm going to really try and be a bit more understanding with you people'

– we all exchanged looks of deep alarm. 'Obviously I'm failing in my duty to educate you. So, I propose to try an experiment. I shall let you choose your own lesson, and I promise to undertake a lecture on any subject of your choice. Come on – anything that interests you. Just speak up and tell me what you want.'

He looked around the classroom and there was total, stricken silence. 'Mr Johnson – come along, what about you? Cheeses of the world, perhaps?'

Robert Johnson-from-Sainsbury's grinned and looked for inspiration to Bob Greenhough, who grinned back. Neither of them said anything.

'Miss Babington? The History of the Powder-Puff?'

'Will you really let us have any lesson we like?'

'Anything, *anything*,' said the desperate man, 'if it relates to your Quest for Knowledge.'

'What about Marxism?'

'Ha!' He gave a roar and said exuberantly, 'Marx! Well, he was a typical Victorian father and you wouldn't have got away with much, Miss Sands, if he'd been your father. I shall certainly come prepared next week to talk on Marxism. Now, can you get out your notebooks.'

He had been an engineer and now he had a farm, where he spent his time when he wasn't part-time teaching, so I guess he liked to meddle in everything, and was game to take a class on Marxism.

'Here,' I said to Fiddle at the Branch, 'did you know Mr Cox is going to take lessons on Marxism?

'Really?' said Fiddle, sparking up. 'Old Coxy,

heh? Well, next week I'm going to bring up the subject of the teacher's role in society, and see if we can get a discussion going on the Cuban educational programme and what they're doing in the Maoist countries. They send their students into the countryside, to the people, so they don't get alienated from them. So the students know right from the beginning that they are part of the working class and aren't in some special class of their own, that they owe the money for their education to the sacrifices of the workers . . .'

'Tell us about Marxism, and we can surprise Mr Cox,' demanded Jennifer.

'Er . . . well . . . the basis of Marxism is the dialectic, and er . . .' I floundered.

'No, dreamboat, don't tell me now or I'll only forget. Tell me just before the lesson.'

'Well, if I can remember. We'd better get Fiddle to write it down. But in any case, we ought to have a democratic committee, where everybody votes and you can change whatever you like.'

'Do you mean – if we all vote for it, we can get Mrs Shaw to make her treacle tart every day?'

'Yes,' I said rashly.

'Goody, it sounds totally jammy. And we can vote for more lemon sponge, and she needn't cook cabbage ever again.'

'Yes – and you can be the one who tells her. *If* you dare,' said Ann.

'Well anyway, I don't see how we can do that because cabbage is good for you, and we'll need all our strength,' I said, trampling on the threatened excesses.

On Tech day we were all in sober chastened mood; now that we were getting what we wanted, nobody dared laugh or be late. We sat waiting in the classroom.

'I don't mind learning about the dialectic,' said Val graciously, 'just as long as you remember, Sylvia, that this is the best country in the world.'

'And we've never had it so good?'

'Well, we haven't. Just you name me one time when they've had it better.'

'If we were Tudor princes we would have got a better education.'

'There are a lot more of us than there were of Tudor princes. We can read and write and we've got jobs and food in our stomachs,' Val pointed out. She said she agreed with Mr Macmillan, that the Class War was obsolete. 'And I think it's a bit much that you wanted to do Marxism, so we're having that and we're not having anything from the other side,' said Val, in an aggrieved tone.

'Well, why didn't you say something when he asked? Tell him when he comes in.'

'I don't want that, all I'm saying is, it isn't fair . . .'

'Mr Cox,' I said as soon as he came in, 'Val wants us to do the Thoughts of Mr Macmillan.'

Mr Cox left his desk and came over and looked at her as if she were mad. 'What did you say?'

'Nothing,' said Val in a low voice, treating me to a furious look.

Mr Cox began his talk by describing the Marx household, their poverty, and Marx's daily walk to the British Museum. He made much of the suicides of Marx's daughters and of how, scorning capitalism, he yet lived off the proceeds of it, via Engels.

'Now we come to some of his ideas. Although he wrote his work here, I think it's fair to say his ideas are discredited in the West, but they do have an appeal to societies that aren't as technologically advanced or wealthy – Yes?' He stopped politely, as it was Ron with his hand up. 'Surely that doesn't necessarily invalidate them?'

'Well, no.'

'And you haven't said how at the basis of Marxism lies the Socratic method.'

He scowled. 'I was just coming to that.'

'Yes, and what about the Dictatorship of the Proletariat?' said Jennifer.

'All right' – he slammed with his hands flat on the teacher's desk. 'As we're playing at being rational today, for a change, perhaps you can tell me why you come tottering into my class on those things?' He indicated with a wave of the hand at our footwear. 'Come on, I want an answer, not these paranoid glares.'

'Because we're female.'

'Because we like them.'

'Because we're different from males.'

'*Because!*'

'You wear those things to draw attention to yourselves in an underhand manner,' he accused.

We looked at one another and chanted as one girl, 'Yes.'

The following week Fiddle showed Mr Cox the Tanzanian Education plan, which outlined the sending of students to the workers and peasants, as part of their course; but all he said was, 'Fine words butter no parsnips, Mr Middleton.' He seemed to have got bored with asking our opinion.

In Cuba the sugar harvest had been poor and it was the Year of the Economy. In the Retiring Room the *Daily Mirror*, with its pictures of Christine and Mandy toppling the government, was handed about gleefully.

RELIEVING

In the summer after Tech finished we were free to be sent relieving. A list hung in the Retiring Room, the signatures of all those operators who wished to be sent to other exchanges as relief telephonists. The exchanges that were sent operators from Derby were small, old-fashioned ones that the GPO were intending to shut down eventually. So although their traffic level was increasing no new operators based there were to be recruited. The nearest exchange was five or six miles away – Belper, and from Belper onwards they wound further and further into the Amber Valley – Ripley, Ambergate, Somerfields, Alfreton.

Relieving was popular because it was a change, you got paid fares and travelling time even if you did have to be up at the crack of dawn, and in summer it was agreeable to bus into the countryside. The small exchanges had antique yoked headsets and china light-switches, and the boards were like a large version of a firm's switchboard, in that when any subscriber picked up their telephone a disc with their number dropped down into the exchange, and the operators knew exactly who it was, the caller's grandmother's name and who she had walked out with when she was a girl, who the caller was likely to be ringing and – quite often – what they would have had for dinner on Wednesday, as they shared a butcher.

Somerfields Exchange was the smallest, and the most popular to relieve, the mention of it at Derby induced a pleased smile, as of goodies, treats, and scrumptiousness.

'I'm being sent to Somerfields.'

'*Somerfields!* – you jammy devil.'

'Oh, it isn't fair . . .'

'Oh, isn't she jammy . . .'

'Fruit, you'll love it there, the girls are gorgeous and Winnie! – I could just pick her up and kiss her,' enthused Jennifer.

It was spoken of like a convalescent home or the seaside – 'I feel rotten. I could just do with a couple of weeks at Somerfields Exchange.'

The long rocking journey on the bus put you in a half-trance, going from village to village, and roundabout to the first village again, and by the time you arrived you were in a dream. You alighted from the bus, crossed the road, and nearly at the crossroads where the small town began there was the front gate to a little house. It looked just like a little house drawn by a child, with a curvy white path to the front door, set between two windows, a smoking chimney above and a family wash flapping from a clothesline at the side. This was Somerfields Telephone Exchange, and the Switchroom was in the front parlour.

The 'girls' were Winnie, Alma, Mary, and Barbara the Acting Supervisor. They all had soft yielding voices and gentle manners, they lived there themselves and knew the subscribers. The Supervisor was Day Irene; Night Irene lived in the house with her husband and children and took over at six o'clock, after the last operator had left. She was just a name to me, I never saw her. Day Irene was a small dark woman in her mid thirties, vivacious and capable, she was the only one who seemed to fit easily into the wider structure of the GPO. She was often away, acting as Travelling Supervisor for the area. She was active in the Methodist chapel, and ran the Exchange with the same cheerful firmness with which she ran her Brownie pack. Barbara was her deputy at the Brownies as well as at the Exchange, and on the afternoon of the pack meeting they came to the Exchange in their uniforms.

Midway through quiet afternoons Irene would say in an immensely practical, cheerful way, 'Come along now, girls, it's time to lift up our hearts. Mary, leave that call – it's only Mr Potter and he can wait.' Then, Irene's directing fist moving back and forth pushing out the rhythm, they would burst into song: 'Oh yes, oh yes, there is something more/There is something more than gold/To know your sins and be forgiven/Is better by far than gold.'

Thus fortified against despair they picked up their day again with renewed spirits and shining eyes. 'Number, please', 'Number, please', 'Number, please – hello, Mr Potter, sorry to keep you waiting . . .'

Quite often Joan from Alfreton Exchange was there too – she lived halfway between the two places and the GPO transferred her when Somerfields was very busy. She had a fair heavy plait and a tart manner, quite unlike the Somerfields operators.

'Let's send to the shop for buns, girls.'

'Ooooo yes, and some of that gâteau.' Winnie's little brown eyes gleamed.

'If you want *gâteau*' – Joan spat out the word – 'then you'd better get a French person to fetch it. I buy cake. That's good enough for me.'

Equipped with a basket, her thin, dark-coated figure sped out of the gate and down the lane, her long plait skipped behind, much as it had done but a few years before when she was head girl of the local grammar. Winnie looked crestfallen, but Joan eventually returned with iced buns and one slice of gâteau. And how had she acquired this confection?

'I asked for a piece of that soggy cake. Mrs Smithers knew what I meant, she knows I wouldn't use that word.'

'Well but, Joan, it means we've got another word extra in the language, so why isn't that good? It's like a present.'

The Somerfields operators looked mildly on as Joan replied, 'I'm English and I don't have need of fancy foreign words when there's enough English words.'

Gâteau became more and more popular, but Joan was a little walking pocket of resistance.

*   *   *

One particular summer there were two of us from Derby; the other operator was Sandy Atkin. Barbara let Sandy and me take our meal breaks together, and we would wander down a lane away from the town.

'Amazing place, isn't it?' said Sandy, wrinkling her nose.

In the distance cows in meadows floated under the sky. There seemed to be a dream in the air here, it was like one of those places not quite inside time. A tethered goat cropped within the lych-gate, its enamel water-bowl upside down in the grass. We walked slowly to the small plain church, deserted on a hillside. Not many people seemed to come up here, mostly they appeared to go to chapel. We didn't go in the church but sat in the porch on the stone seats and ate our sandwiches under the inscription 'Life how short – Eternity how long'. My mother always made liver-sausage sandwiches for when I went relieving, and she put in an apple and a chocolate biscuit. It was dull land for the most part, there was an emptiness here, like it was the beginning of the world. Over to the east lay land scarred by disused pits, but over the church wall stretched grass with a gold river of buttercups running into the hedgerow, ethereal yellow, heavenly gold.

Sandy left before me because I was on a split shift, which meant arriving early and leaving late and having a longer meal break in the middle of the day. In town you could make use of the time, some girls went dancing, or you could meet up with friends, but there was nothing to do here. I walked downhill to the road, past the goat, who stood looking across the churchyard like a sinner who could never be redeemed. '"Life how short – Eternity how long",' I said to the goat, and it focused its ancient uncanny eyes in my direction and went on chewing.

Somerfields Riddings Jacksdale Hayes Swanwick – all these places were round here merging into one another, but you could never quite make out which one of them you were in. If I asked where I was of a passer-by, the reply would come, 'Well, that's Jacksdale over there,' or, 'You're on the way to Riddings,' or, 'Where are you going to?'

'I'm not going anywhere especially, I just want to know where I am now.'

I started to believe only the inhabitants knew where each place was.

At the Exchange I asked, 'That telephone box – 415 – where is it?'

'It's on the way from the school,' said Alma, cunningly, as I thought.

'Yes, it's on the way from the school, but where exactly is it?'

'What do you want to know for?'

'I don't want to know for a reason – I just wondered where it was, that's all.'

'Well, but you know where it is – you saw it this dinnertime.'

They glittered laughter at one another, the dancing light moved amongst them, from Barbara with her fairygold hair, to Winnie with her little currant eyes and podgy arms, to Mary with her light laughing eyes and leg-irons and bent back, to Alma, of the heavy hips and velvet hair-ribbon and soprano voice that took descant when they burst into song. They laughed and the same light moved between them and they were as one.

Winnie suddenly had a new interest, when the GPO sent an engineer to do work on the lines. 'I'm going to take Ernest home with me and feed him up,' she announced, with a little sigh of contentment, and you could see that her present idea of utter bliss was to feed a visiting engineer with her special plum duff, or whatever it was (Jacksdale tipsy trifle? Riddings roly-poly?). The other operators lifted their eyes to heaven as Winnie prepared to rush off, to cook for Ernest.

'Ernest is like the rest of us,' said Joan irritably. 'He came into the world alone and he'll go out of it alone, and he doesn't need you fuss-potting over him.'

Even Barbara remonstrated softly. 'Winnie, you're being very silly about Ernest. He can get his own tea, he's big enough.'

'Aaaaaaah – you don't understand, poor Ernest has lost his wife; it's alright for you, Barbara, you've got your John,' and Winnie's tiny brown eyes filled with tears. She had been a switchboard operator here as a girl, and over the years had returned on and off, between bringing up a family. You could see she had been what they used to call an incorrigible schoolgirl, and now she was an incorrigible granny.

She wore the same marcelled hairstyle that she probably wore as a young operator, and you could imagine her in long beads and t-strapped shoes.

'Did you used to go to tea-dances, Winnie?'

She chuckles. 'Tea-dances! Ooooo, yes. We did have a lovely time . . .' She was still having a lovely time; they went to chapel teas and outings and choir.

Irene had a traditional GPO voice, the others spoke with soft, dove-like Derbyshire voices, quite different from Derby voices, very attractive – voices that would surely have healed the sick. Barbara, that year a bride, looked like a fairy doll come suddenly to life, with her cloud of flaxen hair and delicate rosy complexion. She was the youngest there, so I don't know why she was so senior – probably the others had dropped out to have their children and returned at the bottom of the seniority list.

'Have you got a union – ' but even before I'd finished the question I knew what the answer would be.

'Oh yes,' said Barbara, 'Irene runs the union.'

'And you do it when she's not here,' I added.

'That's right.'

The facilities for listening in to calls were different at small exchanges. The operators couldn't do it, unless they wore one special headset, which was kept for emergencies. Winnie liked to listen to a schoolboy ringing his girlfriend in the afternoons; she sat chuckling and periodically her mouth went into a little aghast o.

Barbara decided to put a stop to this, and locked the headset away in a cupboard. 'Noooo, Winnie, that's not for you to use, that's for the supervisor,' and Barbara turned the key sharply in the lock and put it on the chain at her waist.

'Aaaaah – it's not fair. It's not doing any harm. Who would have thought when you were a little thing and I used to see you walking up Lazars Lane with your mammy you would have grown up to be so cheeky to me,' bewailed Winnie, turning from the boards and swinging her legs.

'Now then, don't be so mardy, whatever will these young ladies from Derby think of us . . .?'

That summer Sandy and I criss-crossed one another; sent by the GPO first to Alfreton, then to Somerfields, our stints at these exchanges overlapped. One morning had been particularly busy, Barbara had been implementing Traffic Control procedure, which meant logging all information. The GPO had decided they wanted the volume of traffic assessed, probably to decide whether or not to send more operators or to pull us out. We went for our mid-day break, walking along the lane and up the hill, to the deserted church. The day was hot. Sandy had brought some water in a plastic bottle for the goat. We were both quite tired, as it had been a busy morning.

'Look at that,' said Sandy. 'It's tipped up its bowl again. He must be doing it deliberately.'

'Probably as a protest,' I agreed. The goat managed to look at us and superciliously ignore us at the same time.

'What will happen to him eventually?'

'Oh lovey, you mustn't ask questions like that,' said Sandy, whose father was the sub-postmaster in a village, so she was quite used to the fate of animals.

'It seems a shame, to keep him on a rope all his life. In Ancient Greece the goats roamed free. I mean, I believe in Liberty.'

'Yes, I know. I do too.'

'We could just let him off, just for a bit.' I tugged at the rope, but it was thick and firmly knotted. There were nail scissors in my handbag and I started nibbling at the rope with them. It took ages, the rope frayed slowly and gave way, and Sandy urged me to hurry up.

When we got back to the Exchange the discs were flapping down madly as the calls came in from all over Somerfields, reporting that Jackson's goat with its rummaging yellow teeth had visited their premises and destroyed washing and flowers, had overturned bins and frightened small children. He had butted three people, stolen meat from a butcher's basket on a doorstep, and was last seen by customers in the Dog & Doublet clattering down the road to Hayes.

'Wait for it – 312 will call any minute now,' said Barbara, fatalistically, it seemed to me.

'Why will they?'

'Because it's Four Corners Farm, and they've a couple of nannies,' she answered practically.

'You'd better give them a ring,' said Irene.

So this was Somerfields, the favourite exchange.

RELIEVING

The days there were long and warm, and by the time you arrived home in the evenings it was too late to go out, you ate and went to bed, too tired even for dreams.

A MAN AND HIS WIFE

'Now,' Miss Armitage had said during Training, 'when you meet people outside, if, in the course of conversation they should pass remarks or ask you whether you listen in to calls, you are *not* to be on the defensive. Do you understand? You are not to apologise about it, you must say straight away – Yes – that is part of my job . . .'

'Do you listen in to calls?' was quite a usual question to be asked. A GPO operator was supposed to monitor telephone calls to make sure the subscribers were speaking, but not to listen to the conversation. If you did hear it, you weren't supposed to disclose it to anybody. In the highly unlikely circumstance of by chance overhearing a crime being plotted, you were supposed to tell the supervisor. People who declare proudly – 'Oh, the Exchange are always listening in to our calls,' are likely to be living in an illusion of their own creating, because most operators are more fascinated by their own lives than the lives of any subscribers. Quite apart from the fact that we had the supervisor's eyes drilling into our backs almost the whole time, we were used to and therefore bored by other people's conversations, probably in much the same way as the girls at Bournville weary of chocolate because they are surrounded by it all day and can eat as much as they like. You might treasure up sentences out of the blue, but usually you hadn't time to stay with them.

Of all the conversations that I, advertently or inadvertently, overheard, I can only remember one. I can hear it as though it happened last month, and feel as though I came to know the speakers well, although they were total strangers whom I never saw.

The call happened about my second year at the Exchange, and in many ways was incomprehensible to me at the time. It was made by a man in a kiosk, and was to an exchange in Scotland. Oban, perhaps, except that the Oban connexion at that time was dicey, very far away and with whistlings and an echo reverberating along it. And this call was clear; although distant you could hear every sigh and sob.

'I'm sorry, there's no reply.'

'Can you let it ring a bit, please. It's a phone-box and she's probably not there yet.'

'Very well.' I came off the line and took other calls, going back when the yellow disc showed in the clear glass on the board.

'Hello, Caller, can you put three shillings and ninepence in the box, please . . . Two shillings, four shillings – thank you, go ahead.' I came out of the line and put the switch back into listening position whilst completing the accompanying docket.

'You sound out of breath.'

'Yes,' a woman's voice panted. 'I had to run – I heard it ringing, I thought you'd ring off . . .'

'Well, how are you?'

They were talking, so I left the call and took another one, snatching a look at the nearest clock – nearly an hour before Andy would come to relieve me.

'Number, please?' Behind, Mrs Lord was on the prowl in her black high-heels, wearing Yardley's Red Roses, which overwhelmed you as she passed. You knew when she was coming, the scent came first.

'Putting you through now, Caller' – connecting, disconnecting, exchanging a quick smile with Ann – while dialling a number which called forth London Valentine.

'You're through, Caller.'

'Have you finished?' – whipping out the plugs. The yellow disc on the call to Oban was flashing and clacking repeatedly. 'Excuse me, your time is up – will you pay for further time?'

'Oh – yes.' He put a further four shillings into the box, and I came out of the line, listening in whilst updating the docket, as you were supposed to do.

'Please – come back soon.'

'I can't.'

'No, I'm not asking you to come right now. Not straightaway. But can't you come soon, duck – I don't know how much longer I can manage.'

'I'm sorry – I can't leave yet. I can't.'

'No. I know you can't. But you will come, won't you, when you can?'

'Yes,' she said half-heartedly. 'I'll come back soon, you've got nothing to worry about, because he's going to leave me,' she said, desperate, despairing. 'It won't last. He'll leave me.'

'He won't leave you,' he said, in a cheering tone.

'Yes. He will. He's bound to.' Silence.

'Yes. He'll leave me alright. Please don't ask me to come back when I've only got this little time with him, it means so much to me, I know it's going to end, I know it is, I know. Don't ask me to come back yet.'

'I'm not asking you to, duck, I'm not, you stay as long as you like, but it's just – things are getting difficult here, your Sheila's been asking after you, and last night your mother came snooping round – '

The woman broke in, passionately bitter. 'Aw, what did *she* want?'

'Just on the snoop, I expect. I told her you'd gone to a friend from work's house. But I don't know how much longer I can keep it up, duck, it's bound to get back to your mother eventually, somebody's going to say something, one of his friends might open their big mouths . . .'

'Oh my God.' Silence.

'You can see how it is. It's getting difficult. Your mother thinks I'm off with a bad back, but I'll have to go back to work soon or I'll lose my job. I'm worried the kids are going to say something.'

'How are the kids?'

'They're not too bad. Carol's at school. I've been keeping her from going to your Sheila's, in case she asks her anything. Michael's here, he's alright. He hasn't had a bath for a fortnight, he stinks rotten. Honestly, duck, I don't know how much longer I can manage. Mikey, come and say hello to mammy.' A crash and some fumblings.

'Oooo – Ma-ma – bababa?'

The woman's voice changed. 'Hello, my love. Hello, my darling. Are you being a good boy for Mummy, Mikey? Are you, my precious?'

'Aaaaah, ma bubba Mama?'

'There's a good boy. You are a good boy, aren't you, Mikey? You are. Tell me all about it. Tell me, Mikey.'

'Brrrrr . . . sussussuss . . .'

'That's right. Good boy. Bye-bye, my love. See you soon, my darling.' Waves of sighing travelled the length of the land, as the woman cried.

'Hello. Are you there?'

Sniff. 'Yes'– unwillingly.

'Come back, duck. Can't you come back soon . . .?'

The woman's voice rallied in desperation. 'It won't last. It won't. Please don't ask me to come back when it's the only time in my life anything like this has happened to me. I *can't* come back yet, don't ask me to.'

'It's alright, duck, it's alright, don't you worry. Don't worry. Don't get upset. We'll manage a bit longer . . .'

The smell of Red Roses was getting nearer, and I took another call. By much moving of hands and scribbling of dockets, you could to a limited extent simulate busyness, and I went back to the call as soon as possible. There was silence on the line.

'Do you need anything?' he asked, as you might enquire of an invalid, delicately.

'No. He's – he's quite good to me.'

'Oh. Right.' Silence.

'Thanks, duck.' This was the first time she had used an endearment to him.

'Just let me know if you do, anyway. Look, I wouldn't ask, but I don't know how much longer . . .'

Suddenly Red Roses overwhelmed me. 'Take that call, Miss Sands,' spat Mrs Lord, a dissatisfied brunette with amber eyes, sulky like a cat. She should have been a filmstar, but it wasn't our fault she wasn't.

There was silence on the line when I returned to it. Then: 'We want you back. We want you back – you know that, don't you.' Silence.

'Are you there?'

'Yes,' she said, as part of a sigh. She sounded a long way away now. Silence trembled down the line, so that you could hear the equipment contorting and whining.

'We need you, duck, we want you safe back here . . .'

She said desperately, 'I don't know why you're keeping on at me, there's nothing I can do. I can't leave him.' She tried again in one last desperate burst. 'He'll leave me, he's bound to. And when he does that, I don't know what I'll do.'

'You'll come back then, won't you?' he said eagerly. Silence. 'Won't you?'

'Yes.' She didn't sound as though she meant yes.

'You will, won't you – we all want you back home – are you there?'

She sighed again. 'Yes' – she sounded as though she had all but disappeared, there was just a thin voice left, curling into the air and away.

'Listen to me,' he said urgently. 'We want you back. Do you understand? We want you back here. The minute he leaves you, don't you think about anything. Not anything. Just walk straight out of the door and go to the station. Can you hear me?' he said frantically. She didn't reply. 'Don't do anything silly. Don't you stop to think about anything, never mind about the times of the trains, just go straight to the station – the train will come and when it does – you get on it. Don't bother if you haven't got any money, you tell them your husband will pay when you arrive. Do you understand? Can you hear me?'

'Yes, yes,' she answered wearily. Silence.

'I don't know, duck. I don't know.'

Andy Johnson came to relieve me, so I could go for my tea-break.

'Andy, please don't disconnect this call, it's a couple and they're in a lot of trouble.'

Andy furrowed her brow, looked at me and at the call and said suspiciously, 'We'll see.'

'Andy, their marriage is splitting up.'

'Well, we can't do anything about that,' said Andy roundly. 'Oh alright, alright – I won't disconnect them. You get off now.'

Fifteen minutes later I returned to the Switchroom and looked eagerly for the call.

'They've gone,' she said. 'Don't look at me like that, I didn't disconnect them, they got fed up and put the receiver down. They kept repeating themselves,' she said energetically. 'They were just wasting each other's time.'

Andy wasn't an unsympathetic person – one time she sat on the boards for over an hour trying to persuade a caller not to commit suicide, whilst the engineers worked to trace the connexion and the police waited for the engineers to tell them where to go. Afterwards in the Retiring Room she was pink and glistening with perspiration and exhaustion, and Miss Armitage hurried in with a cup of tea for her.

'Are you alright, Miss Johnson? You're to take a double break.'

The other operators solicitously enquired after her as, one by one, they came through the door, their headsets round their necks or slung over their shoulders.

Well, you must just fill in the rest of the story for yourself. Did she stay with her lover? The relentless pessimism in her tone didn't seem to suggest a happy outcome for the affair. But perhaps she changed when she was with him. Did she pull the plug on both alternatives? The almost disintegrating voice seemed incapable of decisive action of any kind. Perhaps she returned and they carried on their life together, and no one knew except them. The toddler would hardly be aware of it, the little girl would forget, the teeming streets around them wouldn't notice or care, her absence would be reflected in no statistic

Perhaps it would come to be as though it had never happened.

On a Saturday, when access to the files was easier, I checked the number of the calling telephone, and found it was one in a line of kiosks outside a branch library, near where I live now. At seventeen I couldn't understand the faraway voice of a woman made numb with passion, who faithfully returned to a telephone box to get news of her family, and a man whose care for his wife caused him to protect her right to love, even from her own mother. I could hardly understand it, but wondered and remembered. Every time I pass the boxes I think of those two, their voices calling from the dust, powers that have lost only their bodies . . . Their story hangs in the air, timeless, unresolved.

LEAVING HOME

It was just after Easter and I sat in the deserted Retiring Room sipping tea and watching sunlight on the stretch of leaded roof beyond the window. There was a flap of wings outside, where scads of pigeons roamed the roofs. It was Saturday, the radio had shot Saturday Club over the empty room but it was just past twelve now and silent, and the flame under the water-heater flickered away to itself. In came Elly, and parked her basket on a chair.

'Hello, Elly, I didn't know you were on today.'

'I'm not, but I'd got to come into town anyway and I thought I'd call in.' And then she sat down at the table and slowly burst into big wet tears.

'Whatever's the matter? What is it?' It was obviously something dreadful, she was crying now so badly.

'I've just come from the doctor's,' bubbled out of all the tears. 'I've just come from the doctor's and – ' Another great tear-laden sob split her face, and I looked round, panicky, for someone else.

'What did he say? Is it something serious?'

Elly was gasping, and she nodded her head, and then started sobbing again.

'Well, it can't be so bad, can it?' But it was, it must be, it looked as though it was something really terrible, some awful life-snatching disease. 'Elly, it can't be anything really awful. Can it?'

She nodded her head that it was.

Avril came for her break; she was older than we were, she might know what to do. 'Why, Elly, what is it – what are all these tears for?'

'I'll fetch you a cup of tea,' I said, and bolted.

'There, look – Sylvia's brought you some tea and I'm going to give you an aspirin, and then you can tell me all about it,' said Avril comfortably, scratting about in her bag for the aspirin bottle. Elly was wiping her eyes now.

'I'm nineteen minutes late back on the boards,' I said. This was a long time.

Elly shot me a hurt look but Avril waved me away with, 'She'll be alright.'

'Miss Sands, wherever have you been? You're over twenty minutes late.'

'It's Elly – I mean Miss Hurst – she's in the Retiring Room and she's . . . she's . . . ill. I think.'

An alarmed Mrs Royle said briskly, 'Miss Arnot, will you supervise, please,' and hurried straight out.

On Monday it came as a surprise to learn that Elly was going to have a baby.

'Aaaaah – her first boyfriend, too,' lamented Freda, 'it is a shame.'

'She's apparently very upset.'

'Oh dear.'

'She's frightened.'

'Well, she's only a little thing and nine whole months . . .'

Susan said Mars is nine months away.

Barbara said, 'I'll never forget when Helen told us she was pregnant – can you remember? – she came straight into the Retiring Room, just tossed her coat into a chair and announced matter-of-factly, "Well. That's it, girls – I'm in the Pudding Club and he's married."'

Helen sometimes brought Victoria in to show her off; she was jogged up and down and presented with biscuits.

'Hello, Torie – gosh, she looks like you, Helen.'

'Look at her, hasn't she grown . . .'

Victoria gazed back at all the crowings with steady brown eyes, and shot out a quick paw for the biscuit.

I wondered how Joy had greeted her pregnancy, after she had been left with me, a little souvenir of the US Army. Her boyfriend was supposed to have come back and tried to see her, after I was born, and I imagined him waiting patiently outside the Exchange in the evenings with the other males. But now I don't think he came back; Joy was just keeping her end up by pretending.

'Is it the boy who wrote the verse on your birthday card?' I asked Elly, and she nodded solemnly. Ellaline – Sweet Sixteen – Dancing on the village green – I'm in love with Ellaline.

'Never mind, lovey,' said Nell in her cosy voice, 'you'll soon have a nice little baby to take care of.'

Outside the Retiring Room window the early summer rain sloshed into puddles on the tarmacked roofs. From a distance across acres of roofs you could see the cathedral and the top of the Strand, the whole town awash in water, spilling out of the sky. It seemed as if it would never stop raining. Everywhere must look the same as it did when Joy was here; she had stared across these same rooftops over a burgeoning stomach. I was choked by a sudden melancholy. Our fads and fancies – the tapestry dresses, the eyelash curlers and friendship rings, gondola baskets with hug-a-bug babies chained to them – all would disappear in just a few years' time. Just as the powder-compacts and pearls, the Fortune chocolates and Dubarry's Heart-of-a-Rose in pink smoked-glass bottle, which had brightened the days of Joy and her friends – all had vanished. And the very first switchboard operators – did they keep violet powder and fur muffs in their lockers? Did they rush to the Switchroom clutching bags holding fans and postcards from the Front? The very daring ones speeding to work on their bicycles, a wonder to the other girls, just as Flora and Anita on their Lambrettas were to us.

'Come on, Dormouse, what's the matter?'

'I was just wondering about these lockers – they look terribly old. Do you think they belonged to the first switchboard operators?'

Betty laughed. 'Fruitie, I'd be surprised if Miss Noah didn't hang her headset in one of them.'

Elly was the prettiest bride you ever saw, with her shoulder-length, smooth hair and broderie anglaise

102

party dress and white flowers. She walked to church between her parents, looking like a little girl on her birthday.

At the Branch we were having some difficulties. The Young Socialists' Easter Conference had passed lots of resolutions which the Labour Party apparatus hated, and now they were planning to proscribe all independent newspapers.

'We'll have to be ready for them,' said Rick, 'and plan our course of action before they strike.'

We called a special meeting of supporters, and it was voted to change the name of the paper every time it was proscribed, so the Party national executive committee would have to go through the whole process of proscription each time the name was changed.

Fiddle of course was immensely delighted. 'The Labour Party's a reformist party – always was and always will be, and you're wasting your time and deceiving the workers by giving credence to it.' This was Fiddle's way of saying I Told You So.

Anyway, we had all summer to think about it, because there were no meetings then, and it was more difficult to sell papers.

Every month I went to the bank to send fifteen shillings through a credit transfer to *Young Guard* editorial board. Miss M. Spooner, wearing a colossal diamond on her hand, sorted through the little collection of heavy pennies and grubby postal orders for two shillings and threepence, or three shillings, all sent in from outlying districts. This was Maureen. We smiled slightly at one another but didn't speak. Her ring was huge because she had made a catch. I knew this because my mother knew her mother.

'Oh Ruby – you should see the size of the house . . . and for her birthday he gave her a . . .'

'*No!*' my mother would reply excitedly.

'Well, she's made a catch there, Ada.'

They went on like this for ages, sounding like silly young girls from a different era, which I suppose is what they were.

'You and Mrs Spooner are ridiculous when you get together. You sound like a right pair of silly articles.' This is what *her* mother used to call her.

'Oh do we? Well I might tell you Maureen Spooner is a clever girl, she's got her head screwed on tight . . . And what time was it you came in last night? It's about time you started acting responsibly . . .'

I started knitting a matinée jacket. Elly and I didn't bump into each other much, although we still shared a locker. She seemed to decrease rather than increase with pregnancy; she was very quiet and was often unwell. 'What's happened to Elly?' I asked Jennifer how she was. In the autumn she was off sick a lot, and had the baby at the beginning of December.

Lessons finished early at end of term Tech; the girls exchanged small presents, pots of nail varnish or scented soaps, and we all signed our names on a card for Mr Christian.

'Come on,' said Jennifer, 'let's go past Storks. I want to get something really nice for Elly.'

We oooohed over the babyclothes, then saun-
tered through the crowds, and ended up drinking
angels' kisses in the Spotted Horse. The boys had
got there before us; Noddy and Robert Johnson-
from-Sainsbury's were exchanging reminiscences of
all the different drinks they'd ever had at Christmas,
Bob Greenhough was in the Gents' being sick.

Ron came over and asked to taste one of
our drinks and then made a face. 'I think it's
the sort of drink girls like,' he said cautiously.

Christmas week on the boards was very very
busy, the Switchroom was well-lit in the dark afternoons and all the calls lit the boards dazzlingly and
non-stop; as fast as the switchboard operators took
calls more calls came winking. The Switchroom
was ablaze with them. The traffic was so heavy
that two aberrant males were dragooned in from
the night staff. The Dining Room was packed
with postmen tucking into bacon and eggs round
the clock. The Canteen served slices of turkey
with brussels sprouts and roasties and thick slabs
of porridgy stuffing, and a gravy extraneous to
everything else on the plate. In the Retiring Room
Sal and Pamela were hanging garlands. I borrowed
a shilling from the *Young Guard* sales tin, to
enter the Union Christmas Fuddle, run by Sal.
On the table was a box of chocolates laid out
in beribboned heart, sent us by a subscriber,
and above all the noise, 'Oooooo, which one's
the strawberry cream?'

In the Switchroom Victoria's shrieks split into the
heavy buzzing air, as the present she had brought in

to hang on the massive Christmas tree was prised from her fingers. Chris came tottering along the corridor, swinging her headset; red pom-poms from the ties on her dress flew about before her. Unwrapping a book – *Windsor Castle* by Harrison Ainsworth – Merry Christmas Love from Jennifer. Chris and I went a forty-minute dash from the Spotted Horse to Jimmy's to the Saracen's Head, as it was a special occasion drinking Cointreau and – Chris's favourite cold-weather drink – brandy and Babycham.

The GPO sent taxis for us at Christmas, and the shifts were half-day ones. 'You see, we have to be on duty all the time, because otherwise the town wouldn't be able to manage on its own,' I told the Branch.

'My, we are important,' said George Hall. I *completely* ignored him because, actually, I thought we were.

In the market square next to the war memorial stood an unwieldy and slightly raggy tree with bright empty parcels – somebody always pulled one off and opened it, to reveal an empty shoebox; crowds milled about and people stood singing 'It came upon a midnight clear' and as the afternoon darkened lighted buses rattled homeward. At the holiday and afterwards the square was empty, except for the snow that was wished for at Christmas, flakes hurling about, trapped in the square as in a snow-globe. The silent clock, the white sky darkening early, the bleakness of the year starting all over again.

Easter saw another bust-up with the Labour

Party. Rick had important exams but I went to YS Conference, and then Aldermaston.

'Oh glory,' said Gillian, 'I've got Mrs Benjamin.' We exchanged looks. She was known to all the switchboard operators. She would ask for a number and then try to engage you in conversation because she was lonely.

'Hello – the number is ringing for you.'

'Is it? Thank you, but you have no idea – I'm ringing my relations but they don't care about me, I don't know why I'm bothering. What can I do – do you know what I can do?' She shot these questions straight at you and waited for a reply. We didn't call her by name, and she knew none of us by name, but she had been ringing in for years and was well known. Some operators were quite needlessly curt with her, but many were sympathetic, the young ones more especially, perhaps because she was new to them but also when you are young you have more faith you can help someone, even a little bit. In the afternoons when it was less busy Ann could be heard cooing, 'Did they? Did they? Aaaaaah – well, never mind, try not to think about it . . .' or Jennifer would sit chatterboxing to her about new clothes and hairstyles; Judy and Kath spoke kindly to her, and Janet sat telling her about Woodentop, her kitten.

'Oh dear, you sound *such* a little girl, life's *so* cruel, darling, it will *destroy* you . . .'

'Sorry, there's no reply.'

'Try them again, darling – they know it's me ringing and they're not answering.'

This seemed very possible, but I said, 'Very well, I'll dial the number again.'

'You've no idea, I just sit in this house all the time, nobody cares, they're all too busy, I don't know what to do with myself.'

'Well, why don't you go to the pictures? – What's on at the pictures?' I mouthed aside to Chris.

'Thank you, Caller – you're through. *Midnight Lace*.'

'Hello – *Midnight Lace* is on at the Odeon . . .'

'Darling, how would I go there, I can't go there.'

'Yes, you can, if you go to a matinée it's quite nice, lots of people go on their own in the afternoons, and you can get yourself a bag of toffees.'

'No, no, I can't go . . . no, I can't.' She obviously wasn't going to the pictures, she really only wanted to talk. She spoke in a sloshed sort of slow drawl, but when speaking on a connected call, her voice quickened and sounded brisk. So maybe she was half-impersonating drunkenness to give herself the courage to speak to strangers.

Mrs Benjamin was married to Stanley Benjamin, the gentlemen's outfitter. His shop had been there for years, with swathes of tweed and suiting looped across its windows. Next to it was Lady Anne, a gown shop. As small children, we had watched the contents of the window change each week, and laid claim to the prettiest dresses – 'Bags I that one.' 'No, I bagsed it first' – the plaster models with their faceless faces and gathered dresses, trim and ladylike. The mini skirt never put in an appearance there. We knew Mr Benjamin was the tailor and Lady Anne was his wife. The shops even had an archway inside, joining one with another. Lady Anne had her own carrier-bag, with her name written as a signature. None of us had seen her. We saw him sometimes, little and hunched, going outside his shop with a long pole to pull down the canvas awning when the sun shone.

It was strange to think that Mrs Benjamin, demanding and querulous over the telephone, was the Lady Anne of childhood fantasy. 'I thought Mr Benjamin was married to Lady Anne – that the dress shop was called after her,' I said to Faye on the boards.

'Oh I think it's just a name,' she said.

As Lady Anne was fleshless, so was Mrs Benjamin to us, for we never saw her. Yet with all her demands she seemed very bodily present. I imagined her with flashing expensive rings and perhaps a white stripe in dark hair.

'Hello – are you there? Do you know of anything that will get out a stain? I can't ask them here, they won't be any use to me, darling, and I can't get it out . . .' The voice was breaking. 'What can I do? Do you know what I can do?'

'What is the stain?'

'It's Chartreuse, it's completely spoiling everything . . .'

Chartreuse. I'd heard of it somewhere. Was that what Noddy was talking about at Christmas when we were comparing the different drinks we'd had? He'd called it green chartoos.

'This Char . . . this stuff, is it green?'

'It was, it's not green now, it's such a mess, it's on figured brocade and I can't get it out, I'll never get it out . . . What can I do? What would you do?'

'I don't know, I'd put it out for my mother to wash.'

She started to cry, so I said, 'Well . . . er . . . if it's pretty material, can't you cut it up and make cushion covers?'

'Cushion covers!' she shrieked back. 'Well, I don't know, I'll ask around and ring you back if I find anything.'

In spite of her difficult manner, when we took industrial action Mrs Benjamin was one of the few subscribers to express enthusiastic and unqualified support. 'I'm all behind you with this Go Slow,' she said. That was what the capitalist papers called it.

'Work-to-Rule,' I replied.

'Yes – you have all my support, I think you're all worth every penny, darlings, and I hope you get your pay rise.'

When the Union had voted to Work-to-Rule, in furtherance of a pay claim and for a reduction in hours, we went on marches and open-air meetings and demonstrations with banners. We went on a coach to a huge meeting in Nottingham market-square, and Tom Jackson came to speak. Working-to-Rule meant withdrawing goodwill and sticking rigidly to the rules – meticulously observing all operating procedure, always looking up dialling codes, although of course with frequent use we often knew them. The effect was to slow down the speed at which calls were answered and connected.

We answered all complaints with the chant 'We're Working-to-Rule'. 'You're Going Slow,' shrilled back the subscribers.

The Post was working-to-rule too, it was joint action; the telegraph boys checked their motorbikes with great precision each time they used them, the postmen went through set procedures like compulsives.

> Postman, Postman, don't Go Slow
> Be like Elvis – go, man, go

and suchlike mottoes were penned on envelopes. It was a chance for everybody to add their little mite and participate in a national happening.

About three weeks into the dispute, I was given a P.18 for having a private telephone call on the boards, and suspended without pay. Every morning my mother came upstairs and shouted at me to get up and go and get another job. In the evenings I went off to the Spotted Horse to find out what was happening in the dispute. Richard took UPW leaflets to school, and Fiddle was at the Sorting Office every morning at five o'clock with Mr Rowley, before the mail went out.

At eighteen the weekly wage of the switchboard operators went up to £45 shillings, after the Work-to-Rule. On my eighteenth birthday my parents asked me to leave, because I'd held a party when they were away on holiday. The neighbours told them there had been drinking, and one of the guests had been sick on my mother's favourite geranium.

'How can you have a favourite geranium?' asked the dumbfounded youth who was the culprit. 'I mean, how can you tell them apart?'

'Well, she can.'

Over that weekend I found a bedsitter in a quiet street, about eight minutes' walk away from the Telephone Exchange, so there would be no bus-fares to pay. The room was large and clean and respectable. The single bed had old candy-striped sheets which were changed once a week by the landlady. On the top of the kitchen cupboard stood a Baby-Belling, which took an hour to warm up and nearly another hour to heat food, a plastic washing-up bowl, and a big jug for holding water, which was obtainable from the bathroom. There was a kitchen table and chair, two arm-chairs near the gas-fire, and a sideboard by the window. The wall opposite the window was papered with the most extraordinary two-foot-high bright green parrots, perched in lime-green and turquoise foliage and bursting shocking-pink blossoms. In a drawer were a collection of runcible spoons and fierce-looking forks, and a set of fish-knives with most of the silver-plate rubbed off. Whoever used fish-knives? There was a funny damp smell, and a used candle in a Chianti bottle, which stood in the wardrobe and made me feel depressed every time I opened the door to hang clothes there.

'That's the worst wallpaper I've ever seen in my life,' said Rick, cheerfully appreciative, when he turned up to give me a lesson about Ancient Greece. He sat in the leatherette armchair rocking one big leg with its huge white-plimsolled foot, over the other leg. I had traced a map of the Aegean Sea and put in some of the names, and sat ready to note down what he said. 'Right. Athens in the fifth century . . .'

'Just a minute. I'd better put the pan on for a drink now because it takes ages . . .'

Rick had a theory about Athens being small and England being small, he thought true democracy was possible here, in a way that would be more difficult to achieve in larger units. 'We all live in little worlds, and these little worlds have more reality than the so-called real world. Democracy is only meaningful in a context where people know one another. To the Ancient Athenians democracy wasn't just an abstraction, because in their city-state everyone would have had a place and could relate to everyone else . . .'

Small is Beautiful Make Love Not War You Belong in Your Community – we painted out slogans and mounted them on boards. In Tanzania, in Cuba, said Rick, the educated were not to be siphoned off from the people to form an oppressive power-structure, but were to return to their communities to aid them, in whatever way they could do. Rick was in the final year of his A-levels and was going to Oxford, but he was definitely coming back afterwards.

Richard seemed to have an inner imperative to teach. He went about like a sheepdog puppy compulsively rounding up chicks in a farmyard.

At the Telephone Exchange I kept falling asleep in my break times, coming to with the Retiring Room swirling about, and Chris or Jennifer pulling and smacking at me urgently, 'Come on, come on – wakey-wakey. You're due back on the boards now . . .' Once I went out like a light and fell into Margaret's coffee and got scalded.

Miss Mills, the Divisional Supervisor, came in and rapped out, 'Take her to the Sick Bay and find Mrs Cliff.'

Judy came to attend to the burn, she tipped a bouquet of flowers out of the wash-basin and dunked my arm in cold water. It was cool and quiet up here; the operators sent their flowers here until they went home.

'Now,' said Judy, 'let's see about this 'ere . . . Whatever were you doing to get it?'

'I can't remember properly . . . Val was sticking up for the Government.'

'Well, I can't do anything for you about the Government, but hold out your arm . . . There we are, fruit.' She put paraffin gauze on the burn, and then looked up, warm in the cold room, smiling through scattered freckles and making me think of Danae in her spinning shower of gold. When the Revolution came I thought Judy ought to be in charge of the Exchange.

In the afternoon I plugged into the board and stood winding up my chair. 'Hi, fruit.'

But it was one of Susan's off days, she replied gloomily, 'The entropy in the universe is tending towards a maximum.'

'Oh,' I said, sitting down. 'Number, please.'

'Trying to connect you,' said Susan, and then: 'There's nothing anybody can do about it. –

Have you finished, Caller? – Gradually the whole universe will get colder and colder and slower and slower, until it comes to a stop. I mean, I'm in favour of banning the Bomb, but what about the entropy?'

'Oh,' I said again, trying like mad to care about the universe, the planets all spinning round without let and us spinning round with them, for ever. It made you feel dizzy.

'So if that's what's going to happen, I don't see the point of it all. And another thing – where does the universe *end*, if you see what I mean.'

'Sorry to keep you waiting. – It probably doesn't end. – Putting you through now, Caller.'

Dialling glumly with her biro, she said, 'When you come to the end of the universe, what is it like? How can it be the end, but on the other hand, how can it go on and on?'

'It does go on and on' – I made it up as I went along, because much of Susan in this mood made you feel wobbly inside. 'Mr Simpkins is calling you from Derby – will you pay for the call, please? Thank you, go ahead. The universe must go on without bounds because otherwise how could it be the universe? Unless it bends back, I suppose,' I said, 'in a circle.'

'Yes, but if it's a circle,' she objected – there was no pleasing her at the moment – 'then there must be something else outside the circle to make it a circle. You are through now, Caller, can you put two shillings and threepence in the box, please. A shilling. One and sixpence. One and ninepence.

Two and three – thank you – go ahead. I don't feel very well. I feel sick.'

I wasn't surprised, I felt quite dull inside myself. She rang her buzzer, and the Supervisor sent for Judy to take her to the Sick Bay. 'Now, Susikin, why can't you find a nice cheerful boy to meet up with, instead of all these miseries?' suggested Judy.

Afterwards, in the Retiring Room, she said, 'What a day! This morning it was Dormouse with a burnt finger, going on about Revolution, and then this afternoon I had to see to Susie Cotton, who was mithering about the universe coming to a stop.'

'Yes, I know, but I wish she wouldn't ring people up at two o'clock in the morning about it. My husband's starting to complain,' said Julie. 'We'd had a late night and we'd *just* got off to sleep when that phone started ringing . . .'

Gaily Smith appeared in the doorway and announced, 'Juliebaby, the Meringue wants you.' Julie wound the flex about her headset and went grumbling off with it.

Susan had a bedsitter in the house next door, but we never bumped into one another. She had left home in the middle of an adolescent quarrel with her mother. 'Why did you leave school?' I asked her once, because she went to a very good Grammar.

'Oh well, I don't know – I was just fed up with it. In any case, I've wanted to leave home as far back as I can remember, and you need a job to leave home. When I see the others now, still walking about in their school uniforms, I'm so glad I left – it seems like 100 years ago.'

LEAVING HOME

In the Spotted Horse Chris pondered on Susan's problem. 'Fruit, you don't need to worry about coming to the end of the universe, because what probably happens is – the nearer you get to the edge, the smaller and smaller you become, so you just never make it to the end. So you see you won't drop over the edge – so just forget about it and have a rum and black.'

'Chris-cross, this is supposed to make us feel *better* . . .?'

It was boiling hot. I woke in the night soaking and shaking, and wondering if an asthma attack was imminent. Throwing off the irritating candy-stripes, I sat up in bed and touched my face. It seemed to have bumps and I rushed across the room to the mirror. My face and back were flaming with a virulent-looking plague of red bumps. 'Ugggggh God, I'm diseased,' I said out loud. There was nobody to tell. I opened the window. The little square of the street was still and dark. Everybody was sleeping. Perhaps next door Susan wasn't, perhaps she was ringing somebody up. I wanted a cup of tea but it would take hours. I must get my parameters right. That was what Rick said. 'We've got to get our parameters right, while at the same time acknowledging they are going to break down, in the long term, because everything is in flux.' This made me feel even more panicky. On the kitchen table was a pot of Sunny Spread which was the nearest I could afford to honey – our fad for eating like the Ancient Greeks was easy when living at home – and the wrapped remains of sixpennyworth of chips. The last two mornings before being paid I ate cold chips for breakfast, saved from the previous evening. Unwrapping them, I wasn't tempted to eat them. Taking one last look at the fiery blobs covering my body, I got back into bed and must have fallen asleep almost straightaway. In the morning by the light of day the red lumps had disappeared without trace.

Ronni seemed to me the epitome of worldly sophistication – striding into work in her leather thigh-boots; smoking her way through Union meetings and raising her voice to call out points of order whenever she fancied; snapping up to the Switchroom in tiny high-heels, whistling and insouciantly swinging her headset. But I sat on the boards with 'Sherry Sherry baby' reverberating round inside my head, and if there was one thing I couldn't understand about Ronni it was her devotion to Mario Lanza. It was hard to believe that her male ideal was tubby and ageing – nay, dead.

'I don't care about any of those things, or what he looks like,' she replied, loyal and intransigent, 'I only care about his voice.' She spurned the record-sleeve in the shops and went to a lot of trouble to obtain one portraying Mario Lanza as the Student Prince and not his actor stand-in. 'I go for the real man, not the dummy,' Ronni said scornfully. 'His voice, when I'm listening to it, it *does* something to me.'

On summer nights she went for chaste midnight dips in Blue Lake with Gianni, a seventeen-year-old waiter at La Girandole Ristorante. They had met when Ronni was taken there by one of her fiancés, and had started up a firm friendship when she had gone back to recover a silver bangle which, during the wait before the meal, she had clasped and unclasped and unwittingly left behind amid the cutlery and flowers.

In the evenings Ronni told him about her boyfriends and her holidays and her work, and in his broken English he described his village, even down to the minutest details like the cobbled alleys and the water-tap, the fat priests playing football in their cassocks, the tiny toddling girls in long knitted socks . . . Ronni wanted to hear about it all, because she was planning on going to Italy one day. He lit her cigarettes and watched her blonde hair in the moonlight, and then he sang in a mournful voice, broken and melancholy:

> *C'erano tre sorelle*
> *C'erano tre-e-e sorelle*
> *Cecilia la*
> *Più bella come sa' fa*
> *l'amore . . .*

Ronni sighed and hugged her stole about her shoulders, as though it had turned cold, watching lights on the water and taking puffs on her cigarette, in a vague way deep inside she wondered if a mate would ever emerge from the flux, before it was too late.

> *Passav' un capitano*
> *Passav' un ca-a-apitano . . .*

Ronni had had about four fiancés, but they seemed to sort of disappear, or just not be mentioned any more. Like Chris's theory about the end of the universe – the closer you got to it the smaller you became, so you'd never actually reach the end – so with Ronni's fiancés. The closer it got to the time of the wedding, the less they were mentioned, until it appeared they weren't there any more. It was more noticeable one time when I'd been off sick and then came back.

'Isn't it your wedding this week?' I asked her. Ronni looked at me cluelessly, and shook her head, as though I was batty. 'But . . . I thought . . .'

'I don't know what you're on about, fruit.'

'Did they split up, or something?' I asked Sue Trill after Ronni returned to the Switchroom.

Sue shrugged and grinned and said, 'Don't ask me – I've never understood Ronni.'

The room I was living in was really getting on my nerves – the disinfectanty respectable smell, the parrots got more lurid and unbearable each time I opened my eyes in the morning. The landlady said it was time the room was vacuumed, so I said yes, and thought no more about it. She placed the vacuum cleaner outside my door, but I was in a hurry to go to a meeting and left it. Then she put it directly in front of the door, so it had to be moved in order to pass. This annoyed me. Finally, I arrived back to find the vacuum cleaner had been placed meaningfully right in the middle of the room. It was nearly two in the morning, I was tired, drunk, and furious, and due on the boards in six hours' time. Slamming the plug in the socket I proceeded to crash about the room with the roaring machine, impervious to knocks on walls and the smash as the vac. hit the table and scattered pots. With abandon I scooted about, not at all impeded by drink – in fact, vacuuming the floor when you're drunk is the best time to do it.

Money was becoming increasingly a problem. The room cost fifty shillings, and after stoppages – two lots of pension fund and union dues – my pay was four pounds and a few pence. This left thirty shillings for everything else – food, clothes, soap, fuel, everything. Living at home I was always broke after the weekend, but this was different, I couldn't afford to eat properly. Barley wine cost 1/6d, I got drunk halfway through one glass, and for that you got a fire and company and a pleasant haze.

'Well, I don't want you back,' said my mother, with considerable conviction, 'but if you approached your father in the right way . . .'

'I'm not crawling.' It wouldn't do any good anyway, he couldn't stand crawlers. He hated drink and hire-purchase, and he liked Mr Attlee, British Railways and Tommy Cooper.

It was getting cold, especially at nights, and I couldn't afford to put shillings in the meter. I stopped asking Rick in, the room was so hateful to me I didn't want anyone else to see it, and 'Come in and watch the gas-fire go out' wouldn't have sounded very hospitable.

'Did you know,' I told the Branch, 'the entropy in the universe is tending towards a maximum?'

'Is it?' said Rick. 'What's that all about, then?'

'It means gradually everything in the universe will slow down and get cold and come to a stop. Like in "The Sleeping Beauty" when everything stands still and everybody falls asleep for a hundred years. Only this time they won't wake up.' They exchanged grins, as though it would all be fun.

The waitress arrived with our coffee. It was Mrs Boulton, the mother of a schoolfriend. She cast a benign smile over us, and for a second I thought she was going to say she would pay for the coffee. She did do that sometimes, and it made me uneasy because she couldn't really afford it. She was one of the small number of parents who liked young people, she was always pleasant and when she saw me selling papers she came up and bought one.

'How's Brenda?'

'Oh – she's doing very well. She's still at Marks and Spencer but she's giving dancing lessons in her spare time to earn a bit of cash – she wants to dance full time when she can. And guess who she's going out with – Vince Eager!'

We stared back at her mesmerised, we stopped what we were doing and everybody else at the surrounding tables shut up and gawped and waited to hear more. For a few seconds I thought entropy had already started.

'Gosh,' I said, dumbly inadequate to respond to such tidings. 'Vince Eager!'

The next time we met up in the Gainsborough Rick had another boy with him. 'This is Peter.'

They pushed their satchels under the dark wooden table and this new boy nodded affably, like Rick, huge in a plum-coloured blazer. 'Pete's interested in joining us.'

'We believe in Friendship and Love and Liberty.'

'And in the workers' right to organise and the nationalisation of the banks for the public good,' added Rick, turning in the carved wooden seat with its dark-red leather. The Dutch windows stretched right to the top of the ceiling, the waitresses moved about the coffee-sodden air as they always had, in their shiny black dresses and ruffled white caps and aprons.

'Are you the girl who goes to work?' asked Peter.

'Yes. I'm a switchboard operator.'

'The girl next door has to go on a switchboard at work sometimes – she dreads it, she bursts into tears.'

'GPO girls don't burst into tears on switchboards,' I said scornfully. 'Are you in the same class as Rick?'

'Yes. We're doing different subjects though – I'm doing English . . .'

'We must start living as we want the world to live,' said Rick, 'and we shouldn't concern ourselves with money. The lust for gold in western societies is a perversion. The Ancient Greeks didn't have this unhealthy attitude to money, they only required a sufficiency to live and work and create, the getting of it didn't dominate their lives . . .'

On the glass door the Gainsborough Lady swung

back and forth as customers came and went, just as she had for Joy and her friends, with her tower of powdered hair and pink and green nodding feathers.

DISSEMBLERS

T he summer of the year we were eighteen we stopped attending Tech, having taken and passed the appropriate exam in preparation for changing from temporary status – Temp. Telst., as it was written after each name in the seniority list (Miss S. Sands Temp. Telst, Miss C.C. Cross Temp. Telst.) – to becoming established telephonists. In the autumn we were sent, pair by pair, to Birmingham, to be trained as Directory and Fault Enquiry operators.

We arranged to meet in the milk-bar opposite the station. Chris was late, as usual, even though she lived in Railway Terrace, for heaven's sake. We were wearing our high-heeled slingbacks and identical green corduroy coats.

'Sorry, fruit' – all rush and smiles.

'Listen, fruitie – you haven't got your ticket, have you? Good, because Susan wants to come with us for an outing, if she can get Bill to take her. If she can, we'll get a lift and we'll be able to claim on the tickets.' Any saving like this was wonderful, because we were desperately short of money.

With a grand skid and some hooting they arrived.

We talked throughout the journey; Bill drove looking straight ahead. He was a lot older than us and didn't join in the conversation.

After eating sausage rolls in the British Home Stores and then trying on silly hats, we split up – Susan went off shopping with Bill, and Chris and I made our way to one of the two big telephone exchanges. We would be late but would say we had got lost, which was not exactly untrue. When we arrived, there were operators from all over the Midlands in a big classroom.

We had digs for the week at Mrs Morley's. 'The GPO always send me nice girls,' she said comfortably, unaware of the ignominy of this description in our world. She fetched in plates of salad and cold meat, and told us about her most famous paying guest, Tessie O'Shea. Tessie was a plump blonde comedienne with an infectious laugh, who was fantastically popular in the Midlands, where she was known as Two-Ton Tessie.

'Tessie always comes to me. She knows I'll treat her properly, I know just what suits her. I keep my best room for her . . .' She took away the plates and brought in two large helpings of bread pudding. Chris visibly winced, but it was delicious.

'Chrissy, you're making a big mistake, it's yummy, it's got cherries and sultanas and almonds and cinnamon . . .'

'No, honestly, I *couldn't* . . .'

'Can I have your share then?' and as she nodded I whipped it from the plate and stashed it in my drawers for later.

'Here's the custard, dears, if you'd like some – oh, you've eaten it. Did you enjoy it? I'm famous for my bread pudding.'

We escaped upstairs as soon as possible and set about unpacking. This took twenty seconds, as we opened a huge drawer in the colossally heavy dressing-table, and emptied our suitcases into it as though emptying bins.

Chris tried out the bed. 'Crikey, fruitie, this bed is a bit low – I think Tessie must have got here first.'

We split into laughter, and spent the rest of the time lolling on the beds and giggling, full of youth and high spirits. At ten we were called downstairs for milk and biscuits, and Mrs Morley said cosily, 'I'll just pop up and put your electric blankets on, girls. Mind Tinker with the biscuits, or he'll help himself.' The grandfather clock ticked noisily, we sat chewing and sipping, and feeding biscuits to the dog, whilst upstairs electricity flooded into our beds from the plugs.

'My father won't have them in the house – they're not safe.'

'It's alright – see how lovely and warm your bed is, Sylvie – just try it,' said Chris coaxingly.

'Yes, I know, but I already have electricity in my body and there might be too much if you put them together . . .'

'The plug is out of the socket, so it's quite safe.' I shut up and got into bed but in the middle of the

129

night got out of bed and started to pull the blanket off, just to be on the safe side.

'Aaaaa Whaaaaa . . .? Oh, *God*, fruit.'

'Sylvie, I want to go back to Derby straight from work tonight – there's this guy I want to see. Do you think you could cover for me if I don't get back in time for work tomorrow morning? I'd do the same for you, fruit.'

'Yes, I know you would.' I wished she was doing it for me, and I was having a mad night-time dash to a boy. 'My boyfriend is a bit jealous so I'm scared of him finding out. I can't talk about it because it isn't going to last – I just want to be with him while we can.'

'Okay.'

Off she went after work, into the traffic and rush hour.

Back at Mrs Morley's: 'Christine's aunt isn't well, she's had to go home.' What a lie. If Chris's aunt had been ill, would she have been likely to send for Chris? Hardly. But some explanation had to be offered for Chris's absence, because we weren't sure how much in cahoots with the GPO she was.

'Shall I dry the pots?'

'Oh no – you go and sit down, I don't have my ladies doing things in the kitchen.'

'I don't mind,' I said. The pin-bright kitchen, the dish near the backdoor with DOG on it, the highly polished furniture and knitting cast into the chintz chair, the comfy uninquisitive Mrs Morley – it was like being at a relation's house, and I slipped easily into drying pots, as I would have at any aunt's.

Mrs Morley even wore those check carpet slippers with the cuffs pinned back with tiny buttons, that aunts always wore.

'Are you at a loose end, my dear?' she said kindly, and I didn't like to appear without Inner Resources, so I just smiled. 'If you'd like, after I've put Mr Morley's dinner to steam, I'll show you Tessie's room.' She put out Mr Morley's dinner on a plate and covered it with another plate, and put it to steam on a big saucepan, to be hot for when he got back from his shift. Then she went into the hall and took a key from a bureau and I followed her up the stairs.

'There,' she said, throwing open the door. The room wasn't big or grand, but it was very comfortable in an old-fashioned way. A cushiony easy-chair, a pink bedspread and pink brushes on the crocheted mats on the dressing-table, china candlesticks and matching dishes and pots, wreathed with flowers. Mrs Morley touched everything lightly and lovingly. 'This is the room I keep for Tessie – I got that chair for her specially, to relax in. I don't really like anybody else having this room, but sometimes you have to. There's a nice gentleman who's got it at the moment. See . . .' She picked up a large framed photograph of Tessie in feathers and sequins. Across one corner was written 'To Dear Hetty from Tessie'.

'Come away from there, dear, that's his box – he's a magician and they don't like ladies near their stuff. You see – that's why the theatre people come to me – I know their little ways . . .'

'Thank you very much, Mrs Morley.'

*   *   *

131

Back in the bedroom I sat on the bed, looking out of the window. Wind gusted about the garden, dancing the leaves and swinging the empty clothes-line. Watching the mist swirl I thought of Chris, eyes sparkling above her fur collar, disappeared into the autumn vapours.

Chris and I didn't bare our souls to one another, or often exchange confidences, but kept ourselves in good spirits. Neither of us expected to know what the other was doing.

As nine year olds, we had attended Miss Blair's classes. Chrissy, with her merry cat's eyes, first seen on the end of a crescent of little girls and one lisping little boy, cooing out 'Mooooooon mooooon moooooooon' in unison, to be coaxed into pronouncing our ooooos properly.

'We have a beautiful language and we must keep it so,' said Miss Blair.

Each child had to stand in the corner and say their allotted poem. Rosemary Smith was the best of all; she was thirteen and Miss Blair entered her for Speech Festivals.

' "This is the weather the cuckoo likes/And so do I/When showers betumble the chestnut spikes/And nestlings fly . . ." ' We sat watching as Rosemary sang out in a tremble of delight. She was at the Exchange now, heavily pregnant and waiting to leave, and if you reminded her she had been Miss Blair's best pupil, she became sulky.

At the senior school Chris was a small solid little girl, her hair carefully treasured up into a long pale pony-tail, which whisked behind her as she darted about. By the time we met up again at the Exchange she had grown slender and her smile, exactly the same as it always was, now appeared sexy, situated in a different context.

Her boyfriend, Joe, used to wait for her outside the Exchange. It got so that she didn't want to see him, and the operators going down with her in the lift would get out first and furrow their eyebrows or very slightly shake their heads if Joe was to be seen leaning disconsolately and innocently against the outside wall, and up Chris would go again with the lift.

'I thought you were off at four o'clock?' I said one time, finding her cowering at the back of the lift when I opened the doors.

'Yes, I was . . . but . . . fruit, do you think you could go out and tell Joe I left ages ago?'

'No, I can't. It's your job to tell your own lies. I don't mind letting you know he's there but I draw the line at going out and telling him lies.' As we stood arguing the lift shot up again.

'Please – I am going to tell him, but just this once . . . honestly, I'll be sick if I have to go up in this lift one more time . . .'

'Hello, little fruitdrops – are you stopping the night?' asked Susan Arnot, clanging shut the gates.

'Good evening, Miss Sands. Are you still here, Miss Cross – don't you want to go home?' asked Miss Mills, in her winter coat and iron-grey corkscrew curls, bobbing off home to her mother.

'Christine, it's nearly five o'clock,' I said, sort of outraged.

'Please, Sylvie . . . He's so jealous,' she said, a little gasp of dread in her voice. 'Joe was everything to me, I'd do anything for him, I got asked to leave school because of him, I lied to my parents to be with him. I don't understand. I loved him so much. And now – well, I suppose I don't,' she said, truthful and at sea with herself, as we took off from the ground again.

'Okay – just *once*' – I laid a stern finger in the air – 'I'll tell him you've gone home.'

Outside, hollow-cheeked and bony, stood the infamous Joe, and foggy in the evening the fire-escape lights spiralling round and round, like the stairway to a magic castle.

Honestly, it was quite a good piece of acting, Miss Blair would have been proud of me, because I went past him and then turned back, as though on impulse. 'You're not waiting for Chris, are you?'

He hunched his shoulders away from the wall and nodded, eager and surprisingly boyish. He nodded pleasantly when I said she had left ages ago, he looked back at me and at the tall Exchange, his eyes wandering up to where the lighted steps disappeared into the evening sky.

Chris had said she would tell him it was over, but it was months and months ago and we had never mentioned it again, so I didn't know what had happened and didn't enquire. But I never saw him waiting again, or Chris dizzy in a lift.

Abandoned on the floor in the bedroom lay a discarded shoe, with spectacular curved instep and a hole for Chris's absent toe.

The old dark cumbersome furniture in the room was oppressive. In the drawers should be glass bead necklaces and lavender-bags. In the warmth and the rich heavy smell there was no damp here among these old things. Old books were piled on a tall-boy. I pulled out the *Girls' Own* for 1883 and sat down to read it on the bed, tucking into a fairy-cake saved from the tea table. Full of romances and dress patterns and recipes. I noted down 'A Good Soup to Take to the Poor', but it took so long to cook that the Baby-Belling would eat too many shillings. Next to a recipe for pickling walnuts there was an article on the first female clerks in the Post Office: 'In the early part of 1881, the Postmaster-General determined, with the consent of the Lords of the Treasury, to throw open the appointments in the Savings Bank Department to public competition ... to judge by the opinions expressed and the fears which are entertained one might suppose that to be of the gentler sex was a disqualification for all employment requiring an ordinary amount of common sense,' say the writers of the *Girls' Own*.

'Every effort appears to be made by the Post Office to provide proper accommodation for the ladies in their employment, and the fact that it is intended shortly to increase their number shows that the Government are satisfied with the success of the experiment, and that the ladies employed have made good their claim to the possession of the requisite ability.'

Good heavens, what a fuss! All for an old job that we took for granted. Line drawings of girls, with their manes of fettered hair, clear brows and faces dewy with moral earnestness and eagerness to go out into the world and work. I looked guiltily towards my notes on the bedroom table which I should be memorising. Then I sat reading 'Robina Crusoe, Girl Castaway'. The clock moved round ... as I put the book away a few yellowy snips of dead maidenhair fern made flutters between the pages, and a little cluster of lilies-of-the-valley. Perhaps Eliza Woodhead, whose name was written out on a Certificate of Proficiency also enclosed, pressed bits of her wedding bouquet here. It was gone ten, and I put out the light and went downstairs for milk and biscuits.

Chris arrived back in the middle of the afternoon's lesson. 'Feeling better, Miss Cross?'

'Yes thank you,' said Chris, wisely not elaborating. She rustled her way to the desk.

After tea we settled down on our beds. She was copying out the morning's notes. 'I'm sorry I was late – he said he'd drive me back to Birmingham, but I had to wait till he was ready. Actually, I'd appreciate it if you didn't mention it to anybody. My boyfriend's so jealous.'

'Are you still seeing Joe?' – I was surprised.

'No. That finished ages ago. This is a different one. But he's just as jealous.'

'Well, I won't say anything. Socialists don't believe in possession or jealousy or stuff like that. Jealousy is one of the Seven Deadly Sins, anyway.'

'Well, so is Lust, I suppose. Honestly, Dormouse, you are a fool sometimes.'

A door shut on the landing. 'Don't say Tessie's arrived?' enquired Chris.

'No, it's a man using that room. He turned up late and had Horlicks last night.'

'What about this guy you're keen on?'

'Well, he doesn't live in Derby and he's in a different organisation to me – the group he's in thinks Russia is state-capitalist: the group I'm in thinks it's a degenerated workers' state. So we don't meet very often,' I said, starting to etch in a touching little cameo of thwarted mutual love, which was not the case in reality. 'So you see, he's a state-cap and I'm a workers' statist, and it can be difficult, because our organisations write documents against each other.'

'Okay, fruitie, I get the picture – he's a state-cap but a rose by any other name . . . Can't you pretend you're a state-cap, or whatever it is?'

'No, not really. I read a book called *State Capitalism* and I couldn't understand it.'

'Well, who's that boy you always seem to turn up with?'

'Oh, that's Rick. We're in political agreement.'

Chris sputtered into laughter. 'That's what you call it, is it?'

'Well anyway, what about this guy who's post-Joe?'

'Phil, his name is. I'm probably going to finish with him soon – he's too jealous. He thinks I should do exactly as he says. He gave me a set of really beautiful hairbrushes – tapestry and silver backs. But he makes an issue out of everything; if I'm not where he tells me to be at a certain time, he wants to know where I've been, he checks up on me to see if I'm telling lies. It's driving me insane. After the last row I just got the brushes he'd given me and threw them on the fire. I felt sorry afterwards – for the brushes, not for him. He used them as a way of saying he has the right to tell me what to do. Anyway, we'll see. I probably will finish with him. He's given me some lovely things, but I don't care about that. Well, I did like it at first. It makes you feel as though you're worth something. Look at Susan – Bill's quite good to her. She finds it hard to manage now, but what she'd do without him, I don't know. You manage, don't you?'

'Huh – yes, and I'm starving most of the time, two days after pay-day. That's why I have to take thought for the morrow at the tea table.'

'Susan can be silly with Bill. In one way he'll do anything for her, but in another, she lets him walk all over her. She makes him wait – she made him wait two hours one time while she put on eye-makeup – and she does have other boyfriends, thank God. But it's just . . . she drops everything for him,' said Chris.

'Does he drop everything for her?'

'Well, no, because he's married.'

'Married! – that must be why he's so boring.'

'Gosh, I'm absolutely starving. You haven't got anything secreted on your person, have you?'

'No, I haven't. As we had trifle for tea I don't see quite how . . .'

So we giggled away the time. Dear Chris, with her gilt hair and happy nature . . . dressed up, two little fish skipped on her dress – a birth-sign brooch.

'Oh yes – Pisces.'

'You don't have to say it like that, I am a Pisces really, I'm stuck in the wrong astrological body,' said Chris. Whenever Ronni sat in the Retiring Room reading out the horoscopes from the *Daily Mirror*, Chris sang out 'Pisces' when it was her turn, and the sign did suit her, but I knew she wasn't Pisces because we went to school together. 'I don't care, I can be what sign I like,' said Chris.

On Friday morning we set off for Birmingham Exchange with our suitcases. Mrs Morley came out to wave. 'Bye, dears.'

'Bye,' we shrilled back, waving heartily. 'Rita and Janet are coming next week.'

'Oh,' she said comfortably, shooting a quick slippered foot across the doorway to stop Tinker getting out. 'Well, I'm sure they're going to be nice girls.'

We took off through the autumn rain, past the honesty podding in front gardens and the ragged roses, reciting '*This* is the weather the shepherd shuns/And so do I/When beeches drip in browwwwwns and duns . . .' We stood at the bus-stop chanting, putting in lots of emphasis, as when we first learned it at Miss Blair's.

'Miss Blair takes us for Civil Defence. Why don't you put your name down for it next time, it's dead jammy and we have some fun.'

'Learning how to goose-step, were you?' I said crossly. As Chris never wore any but the highest of heels this idea made us crack into laughter. Then I turned serious again. 'I didn't put my name down, Chrissy, because it's training to practise deceit on the masses. It's lulling people into a false sense of security about the Bomb.'

'Well, it's a whole week off work, fruitie.'

Yes, it was very peeving, and I was trying like mad to think of a good, if hypocritical, reason for putting my name down next year.

PROBLEMS

When we got back, Derby seemed small and dinky after Birmingham, the town's streets narrow, the market place with its eighteenth-century houses like a dolls' town.

It was Wings' Night, and Miss Marriott let us loose in the streets with tins and little pins with paper wings on, to stick on the lapels of donors. We met at the bottom of the steps of the Regal, where a film about the RAF was showing. Barbara handed the tins out, and we had to crash them up and down as the audience came flooding up the steps to the cinema doors. The film was showing all week, but so many operators had volunteered that each one only had to come for one evening. 'Honestly, I'm sure Dolly has a soft spot for the RAF, she always makes such a thing about Wings' Night,' said Maureen. It was felt that she must have happy memories, or maybe sad ones, because of the War.

'Any switchboard operator who turns up wearing jeans or trousers will not be issued with a collecting tin' read the stern words written on perfumed paper and pinned to the noticeboard. 'She wants us dressed up and looking like crumpet, to swing tins at people,' observed Janet.

The Meringue certainly had absurd ideas about dress – she even frowned on trouser-suits, which were newly fashionable. She liked to be abreast of the latest fashion, modified into a crisp bandboxy look. We had been wearing short skirts for ages, but the day after Paris declared that skirts were to be shorter, Dolly arrived at the Switchroom in her suit and jabot, clinquant with gold chains, her skirt now just above her knees. All the operators turned from their boards to look, as she sailed to her desk. She told Pamela Heath, who wore gor-ray skirts and twinsets and real pearls and a diamond ring, because she had married her boss before she got bored and came to the Exchange, 'Mrs Heath – not in the Switchroom please – *so* untidy!' With her pen Dolly made vague motions in the air indicating the cardigan of the twinset, which Pamela sometimes wore round her shoulders like a cloak, the top button fastened. Pamela listened, disdainfully polite.

That week too we packed into the Guildhall to see Miss Blair in *Queen Elizabeth Slept Here*. She had been appearing in plays since just after the War, and they were very popular. Afterwards we went to the Boccaccio, where the coffee was half-a-crown a cup, and it wasn't as good as the Gainsborough coffee, and the cups were very wide and shallow so that it went cold quickly. But the Boccaccio was the in place.

*   *   *

'They're going to blow up the world,' I said to Dr Laurence on my monthly visit.

'They may very well,' he agreed. 'I shouldn't dwell on it, it may not happen for another hundred years, and during that time somebody might think up a way to prevent it. And you will have spent all this time worrying needlessly.' He smiled.

'Yes, but . . . it might happen accidentally.'

'Yes. It might. But every age has its own fears. If you'd lived in the Middle Ages you would be scared of Hellfire.'

'Well, but you have some control over that, and the world at the moment . . . it's awful.'

'Yes. Shall we let the world roll round on its own for a while, and discuss what you've been up to.'

'Well, I've been taking these little green tablets, parstelline or whatever they are, and they make me fall fast asleep and sometimes go blind.'

'What do you mean, they make you go blind? You're not blind now,' he pointed out.

'No, but I will be later. It comes and goes – I can see people's feet on the floor, but no further up.'

'Have you stopped taking them?'

'No, I thought I'd better carry on.'

He reached over the desk with his hand. 'Give them to me. You must stop taking them if they have that kind of effect. There is a place for common-sense, you know.'

Dr Laurence wasn't at all like a psychiatrist in a book, he was cheerful and didn't seem over-inquisitive about your secret desires.

He didn't even make you lie on a couch, although there was one, covered in a bright red blanket.

'Don't you ever make patients lie on that couch?'

'If you want to lie on the couch, please feel free to do so. Be my guest' – he indicated with his silver pencil and amused smile. I sat on it, felt like a fool, and got off.

The only time he was the slightest bit assertive was at the words mother and sister. 'You mean your grandmother' or 'You mean your mother' – it was a real tangle. I recalled that my mother – yes, that's right, my grandmother – never wore perfume, as my sister – sorry, my mother, did – all the time. But she – 'Who?' 'My mother – no, my grandmother – she used to speak of her favourite perfume Black Tulip, which could no longer be obtained. She still had a little bottle of it in her dressing-table . . . 'Who did?' 'My m . . . my grandmother. I can't remember smelling it but I knew it wasn't like the stuff Joy splashed on, she wore White Heather and Fern. Natural, light, ladylike. This other stuff was different, it was heavy and . . . I can't describe it, but anyway, it's a made-up smell because you can't get a real Black Tulip. When I was about three or four, my mother – yes, that's right – my grandmother – she found the bottle in her dressing-table was empty. She went into a violent rage, she blamed me – I hadn't been anywhere near it, it must have evaporated – she got hold of me by the throat and shook and shook, till my father and Joy – what? – yes, sorry, my mother – they pulled me away. My mother – grandmother – she was screaming and crying, and it just went on for hours, till night fell . . .'

*　　*　　*

After a visit to Dr Laurence, I went to the Gains-borough and had coffee and chocolate cake, even though I'd have to make do with a bag of crisps at mid-day, in order to pay for it. But it was necessary. Because there I was, feeling rotten but at least I was eating chocolate cake in the Gainsborough instead of being on the boards connecting calls. Being here in the morning was strange, and I wished like anything Rick or his friend Peter would just walk through the door, and then everything would be different. But nobody I knew came here at this time of day, and Mrs Boulton was too busy to do more than smile and wave.

Collecting the last little crumbs of cake on a damp forefinger, I watched the glass door swing back and forth, and its motion gave an impression the Lady was nodding her head, with pink and green feathers, just as she did at the end of those old films. Why did they all wear white hair in those days; what did it mean?

'Why did everyone wear white hair in those days?' as we sat there the following evening.

'Perhaps they were all trying to look wise,' offered Edna.

'Yes, but does it mean they didn't feel wise enough?'

'They must have been aspiring to be adult, so they must have had a respect for age,' said Rick.

Fiddle said, 'It wasn't everyone who had pow-dered hair – only the controlling class. So it would be spelling out for everyone to see – we are in control, we are the wise ones.'

'But why did they feel they had to impersonate

wisdom? – was it to keep society from falling apart? What was going on then?'

So went the musings in the Gainsborough.

Rick said it was time the rest of us made an effort to give a talk, and not just him and Fiddle. He said giving a talk would give us confidence. David – who didn't need to be given confidence – gave a talk on the History of the Co-operative Movement, the banding together of workers in the last century, in order to purchase food more cheaply and from fresh and unadulterated sources.

'It was a fine example of what workers can do when they get together,' he said. This was a little marred because afterwards he went on to complain that everyone in his office was depressed because the divvy was going up, and they feared this would mean no pay rise. He went on to gripe about his bosses, and said that Alderman Kettle's wife got her dresses from the Co-op free with a nod and a wink. (Whether this was true or just an example of rumour from a disgruntled workforce, I don't know. When I told Joy that Alderman Kettle's wife got her dresses from the Co-op without paying, she fizzed into laughter and said, 'If I wore frocks from Derby Co-op I'd want them to pay me.')

Edna gave a talk on Crown Derby china. The talk only lasted about eight minutes, and she brought some pictures of figurines, mostly pastoral loving couples in flower-decked dresses and breeches, with lacy cravats and baskets of tiny china flowers. She showed the utensils she used, all the different paintbrushes, and we clapped roundly.

Rick suggested I did a short talk on the Post,

so I got a booklet from Mr Rowley, who was in charge of the union, on the History of the Post, and cribbed hasty notes from it, starting with the runners of Cyrus.

It took a large leap of the imagination from the runners, to the post-boys and stage-coaches, right through to Noddy and Jim and Bob Greenhough and Alfie Woodhouse and the other telegraph boys. We didn't see them at work, just at Tech in term-time, and we collected for wreaths when they were killed on their motorbikes, or baskets of fruit if injured. This seemed to happen in spurts; after perhaps eighteen months without any deaths, there would be two boys killed or injured within weeks of one another. Noddy had been seriously injured, he spent months in hospital and still walked with a slight limp. There was the awful day that Gaily's brother was killed. Gaily, in a pink cotton frock put on that morning without an idea of what the summer day would bring, sat grimly taking calls. She uttered a clipped 'Yes' to expressions of sympathy and took another call. In the middle of the afternoon Miss Marriott sent her home.

The Post Office youth club was in the Becket Well Lane building, where the old Telephone Exchange had been sited. The youth club met twice a week, Tuesdays and Thursdays, and they listened to records and played table-tennis and snooker. They were just recently recovering from a big noisy communal fight, when the telegraph boys gleefully chucked chairs about and ended up turning the fire-extinguishers on one another at the end of the battle – the ultimate weapon. Ann and Mavis hid under the billiard table as the foam spewed out over everything, and then they made a dash for the door, covering their mouths.

With a warm smile and a proprietorial air, Ann showed me over, even the kitchen and the broom cupboard. The froth from the fire-extinguishers had dried and spoilt the big main room – it was all over the wooden window seats and the billiard table, the walls and the floorboards.

'The GPO have replaced the fire-extinguishers but they won't do anything about the Club Room, because it's our fault,' said Ann regretfully, shaking her tumbledown curls.

'It's rather a nice room. Better than ours at the Branch. Mrs Partridge the caretaker's wife has pushed us upstairs – it's okay, but it's a real squash.'

'Isn't there even room to dance?' asked Ann pityingly.

'Nobody at the Branch dances anyway, now,' I said, thinking back to the time when we had the big room and, apart from Edna and Graham, girls danced with girls, just as they were doing here, and the boys sat in corners arguing about Clause 4, instead of playing snooker.

'Who has the keys to this place?'

'Sal, probably, as she's on the Welfare Committee. Why, fruitie?'

'I just wondered. It would be an ideal place to put the supervisors when the Revolution comes.'

Ann laughed and pinched me. 'Well, we have to think of these things.'

Who would help, and who would be a liability? The girls in the Tech class would definitely assist, I felt sure. Sal and Pamela, the union leaders, would be sympathetic but very cautious, they'd keep saying, 'We must be careful . . .' Judy wouldn't take sides, but she would be there with bandages. Of the supervisors, Mrs Royle would be indignant and Miss Mills would fly into a panic. Miss Armitage would definitely have to be watched; she would probably try to get in touch with the GPO in London, to take direction, and she would be very resourceful at escaping – with all that Brownie training, she'd be adept at tying knots and tapping out morse. At least the first announcement of revolution would wipe the boredom from Mrs Lord's face.

'I shouldn't count on it,' said Chris.

Miss Marriott would be actively hostile; she knew too many company directors and men in charge of industry in the town, and her sympathies would lie with them. In any case, I didn't think you could quite trust a person who had to wait for Paris to tell her to raise her hemlines. She would have to be locked up separately. The Sick Bay was the best place for her, it was quite nice in there and there were no windows, apart from a minuscule window in the lavatory. Junior could take up trays of food to her.

Ever since the nocturnal vacuuming relations with the landlady had been cool. I paid the rent promptly each week, and regarded further interest on her part as to what took place behind my door as a cheek.

151

Excessive interest in the cleanliness of bedrooms was to be expected from mothers, who charged about £2 a week for full board and laundry, who had breakfast waiting on the table when you flew down in a rush, who served mushroom patties on Thursdays because they knew you were partial to them; who bought you the odd net petticoat or pair of gloves, as the fancy took them.

Wrangling over bedroom tidiness seemed to be a major feature of life as we knew it. In leaving home, it looked as though I hadn't escaped. Sally Croft's mother, in a fit of fury, had packed all her belongings in suitcases and slung them out on the lawn, when she wouldn't clean her bedroom. And Janet had returned home from work to find her mother had taken her tangerine lipstick and written in big bitter letters on the plain paper in a hastily discarded stocking-wrapper 'HI, PIG – WELCOME TO THE STY' and propped it up on the dressing-table.

'I suppose I just dropped it on the floor – you know how you do . . .'

I knew exactly how you did – in bedrooms all over the land girls shot late from beds, found their stockings were holey and, if lucky, tore into an emergency pack, abandoning the wrapper to fall where it would, and raced downstairs to get to work on time. At weekends mothers pushed cans of polish and dusters at daughters and said, 'It's time you cleaned that *dreadful* room . . .'

Girls' rooms – boxes with secrets inside, old dolls, flowered curtains, and the dressing-table, where you laid out your brushes and all implements for constructing the illusion thrown back from the mirror. All the paraphernalia of disguise was there — powder bowl and scent spray, jewellery box, crocheted mats and little china pots, a tin of letters, candlesticks empty but as though ready to hold votive candles to the face framed in the mirror. You put the face there, with the lipsticks and pots of shadow, as though there would be nothing there to reflect unless you did. Slung among the objects of disguise, the topsy-turvy doll, the bride with a witch under her skirts, and the pile of clean underwear that your mother left to be put into drawers.

When my mother had left my clean clothes she always tipped the doll into the bits-of-net bride, and each time I opened the drawers and layered the fresh clothes into them, I reached out and flicked her back into the little witch, with her black skirt and clothes-peg face under steeple hat, her pipe-cleaner arm bent to clutch a tiny corn broomstick.

As a child I had been a very junior partner in Joy's dressing-table, with its blue-glass powder bowl, its glass showing three faces and they were all hers. In those days I couldn't wait, ached to have my own dressing-table. Since leaving home, as an act of vandalism, almost a desecration of a shrine, I heaped high a pile of books on one side of the battered 1930s dressing-table in the bedsitter, dropped newspapers into the pit in the middle, and swung the glass to face the wall, as though the smiling illusion it contained was in disgrace.

Before the cloakroom mirror a line of girls back-combed hair and made up faces. We aimed to look pretty and not interesting. Pink-frosted lips – baby-pink – the supervisors wore red but we mostly wore pink, pink was the fashion, to emphasise eyes, which were sketched in with mascara, pencil, shadow. Looking like a production line of rosebud dolls, girls sketched in the same face, the same mask, many faces were one face, the collective rather than the individual, the particular sunk in the general. Such a being is easier to sustain, when it is one mask worn by all. Almost as though it would be too hard to bear alone. There was a difference in tints, in shadings, but the underlying design was of one Face.

Ronni was twenty-five, she wore scarlet lipstick, she was the only switchboard operator I could think of who had an ambition. Susan had already achieved her main ambition – to leave home. Janet intermittently spoke of applying for teachers' training college, but she always forgot about it. Chris never spoke of ambitions, but perhaps that was because they were tied in with her squeals over babies. The nearest I got to an ambition was a hope that the GPO would hold a competition for a new TIM, because I'd like to have entered and won it. This scarcely constituted an ambition, because you couldn't influence it taking place, only wait and hope. TIM was a switchboard operator called Jean; she sang out numbers and the engineers clicked them into place, into an order, organised them into maths, so we all thought we knew where we were in our hurtlings round the sun. She sang out and then her voice was broken into bits by the engineers, and reset into a pattern.

Chris came bouncing in, arranged her petticoats and sat carefully down to drink her tea. 'How do I look?' she demanded, patting at her hair, now in a french pleat topped with a chiffon rose, 'because I've just come from an interview,' she said, with a smug little smile. 'Guess where?' We shook our heads. 'You know how boring it can get when you're on a split shift? Well, I bumped into this boy I used to know ages ago, and he promised me a drink if I'd go with him to the Labour Exchange and tell them we were married and we'd got five children.'

'Christine!'

'Chrissy, honestly, fruitie, just as if they would believe you . . .'

'So he borrowed somebody's baby and I had to hold it and we said we'd left the other children at home with his sister . . .'

'But you're not old enough to have five children,' said Jean.

Patiently Chris counted out on her fingers, 'One when I was sixteen, one at seventeen, eighteen, nineteen, twenty – and I told them I was twenty-one,' she finished triumphantly.

'But you're only eighteen!' said Hildegard.

Chris grinned. 'They seemed to believe me. I had ever such fun making up their little names. There was Mickey Junior – the guy's name is Mick, and there was a little Christine, after me, and I called one after Sylvie and one after Janet, and the baby was called Ernest, after Mr Marples.'

There was a general shriek. '*Nobody's* going

to believe that, babies aren't called Ernest any more . . .'

'Well, Chrissy, I do think you might have shown some solidarity, and called it Tom, after Mr Jackson.'

'Yes, I did think of it, but I kept thinking of him sitting in his pram with a little handlebar moustache.'

'There you are, Nell, that's a name for you – Ernest.'

'No thank you,' said Nell, over her large lump and clicking needles.

Ann was laughing, but Barbara said, 'You won't get away with it. It was an awful thing to do.'

'Well, I thought I was doing my Good Turn for the day, because poor old Mick hasn't got a job and he hasn't any money.'

'Yes, Christine, very funny,' Barbara said severely. 'I only hope for your sake the Meringue doesn't find out about it.'

'You won't get away with it – you don't look as though you have children, you don't even look married,' said Betty.

Chris stood up and twirled her virginal blue shirtwaister – *all* girls had one – and said, 'But I wore this specially, it's my courting dress – see, it's got buttons all the way down . . .'

'Christine, if you were twenty and you had five children you wouldn't be wearing your courting dress, you'd be wearing jeans with a very stiff zip.'

'Well anyway, I don't care, I've done my bit and I don't have to go there again. He bought me a drink afterwards.'

'He sounds like a Bad Influence to me,' said Susan Arnot.

It wasn't Ronni who taught me how to hitch, but Irene who used to go to the Branch. Irene was a strong-willed girl with burnished limbs and a high-low voice with a hormonal undertow that sounded like a young boy's voice just about to break; she wore lots of petticoats and was the directing centre of a group of four friends. In the week she was a shorthand-typist at Crumps the Heating Engineers, which was round the corner from the Exchange. At weekends she and her friends left their petticoats behind and went hitch-hiking and youth hostelling. 'You can come with us,' decided Irene managerially, so I did, and it was great. We went to Rudyard Lake and Ilam, and it was fun, sleeping on bunk beds and talking half the night, and cooking in the communal kitchen. I joined the Youth Hostels Association, and they sent back a membership card and a map of Britain with all the youth hostels picked out in red triangles.

We set out in jeans and windcheaters, and we were lucky to get lifts, as there were five or six of us. But it worked out fine. The idea was to hike as well, to see as much of Derbyshire as possible and just enjoy being out in it. We usually took a bus or a train to a chosen point, and took it from there, and hitched back the next day.

After about a year, Irene and satellites stopped coming to the Branch. We bumped into one another after work, between buses. 'It got boring, passing all those resolutions.'

I could hardly believe this. 'But Irene, that's how you change things democratically – if you pass a resolution, it goes forward right to the top of the organisation, and they might take some notice of it.'

'Yes and they might not,' replied Irene matter-of-factly.

I think David was keen on her, he kept saying at Branch meetings, 'I think somebody should chase up Irene Burgan.'

'I'll give you her address,' I said, probably with a shade too much glee because he answered rather shirtily, 'I thought she was a good contact, that's all.'

I started hitching to conferences and demos with Jackie. It was not always possible to attend CND demos and sit-downs unless I hitched. If I had to pay another operator to work for me on a Saturday, it was expensive. We hitched because, although in full-time employment, we couldn't afford the fares and would otherwise have had to stay at home. The best lift we ever got was a coach not on service, going from York to Nottingham. We started to flag it down automatically, as you do everything moving on a main road, realised it was a coach and stopped. But it drew up. Hesitating, in case the driver thought we were passengers. 'Jump on,' he called. 'It's not on service.' It was great because we could move about at will, eat crisps, make up our eyes, walk about, there was no one else around.

The New Year edition of *Young Guard* came out, and there were ructions about it. Everybody knew there was going to be an almighty bust-up, because of the main headline.

All over the country, on banks and council chambers and pub walls, on railway bridges, in red paint, in white paint, poked by fingers in the dust of cars, inked on the covers of school and college exercise-books, was the message HANDS OFF CUBA. *Young Guard*'s first page carried a drawing of Uncle Sam and a Bear wearing a red star, and the words Take Both Hands Off Cuba. All the paper's supporters knew that hell would break loose at the next Supporters' meeting, and they came from all over the land to row about it.

The meeting was in Liverpool, and I arranged to hitch with a girl called Tiger Lilley. We met up on the A52 after work, to hitch all night, hopefully to reach Liverpool in time for the meeting at 11 o'clock on Saturday morning.

Tiger was a bossy little thing with a big bottom; she wore skintight leopard-spot drainies, and she was a Selbyite. Originally she came from Glasgow, where Selbyites came from. We wore jeans and heavy sweaters under our coats, because it was perishing cold on the road at the end of January. 'Listen,' she said, 'it's better if we don't discuss the meetings while we're hitching, because we've got to stick together and we both know we don't agree.' I nodded agreement at this. We met up at six-thirty at Mackworth, and it was already dark. The road was busy, and we got a lift quite quickly. The driver said he was going as far as the motorway and would drop us off there. He asked our names and we told him. 'Tiger, hey? A bit of a wild-cat, are you?' Tiger narrowed her eyes and tried to look feral. I thought she looked stupid but he seemed impressed.

We settled down and started off, and Tiger launched into a long personal history, of her real name, which was incredibly long and fancy, of how she came to have left the family home – she spurned Daddy and his wicked capitalist values and all his money, and Mummy spent her days organising coffee mornings and soirées. The driver, who was a seed rep, for some reason assumed she was an authority on etiquette and started to ask her questions about table manners – all hypothetical because none of us was eating and it was completely dark anyway, apart from lights darting back and forth from the road as cars hurtled and disappeared. The driver's voice droned on, 'I could tell he wasn't . . . quite . . . how shall I put it? Not quite what he said he was, because of the way he ate the jam and bread – he put one slice on top of the other and ate it like a sandwich . . .' Tiger tinkled a refined laugh.

By the time we tumbled out of the car I was at boiling point. 'If I wanted to know anything about manners, I wouldn't ask you,' I said.

'You've got to entertain them. You can't just sit there,' Tiger pointed out.

Thankfully the next lift was a lorry, and he was going all the way to Scotland, so it was past Liverpool. The lorry was beautifully warm, the seats way into the air, with a huge wheel between the driver's and passengers' seats and a heavy smell of engine grease. It was noisy with constant vibration and you had nearly to shout to be heard. Behind was a great white cylinder of liquid oxygen, you could feel its weight as it went tugging along.

The driver was very friendly. 'So what's the big deal about Liverpool – why are you going there?'

'Just for a weekend.'

'No, come on, you can tell me, girls. I pick up all sorts on the road, I don't mind. Are you going for the music?'

'No, we're going to a meeting.'

'Yeh? What meeting?'

Cautiously, we told him, bit by bit and not in too much detail, because we didn't want to start scrapping between ourselves.

'So you think that we should have collectives – well, I meet all kinds, doing this job . . . So what would you do, just you tell me – just you tell me this – what would you do if Russia bombed this country?'

'Russia hasn't bombed this country – the Soviet Union was an ally in the War.'

'Aaaah – no. But what would you do if they did? That's what I'm asking . . .'

He laughed, keeping his eyes on the road. About half past ten we drew into a driveway before a transport café, the driver braked, and the whole thing behind came to a juddering halt. There was a sudden incredible lack of vibration and noise.

'Right. I'm off to the Gents. I'll have egg and chips and two sausages.'

We queued up inside the café, which was startlingly noisy with the jukebox and had checked cloths on the tables. We were glad to be eating, because we had both come straight from work; I had changed into jeans in the GPO cloakroom and stuffed my skirt and high-heels into my locker. We sat munching and the driver collected his meal from us and went off to sit with some other drivers he knew. We had another cup of tea and chatted sleepily, Tiger smoked and I ate a bar of chocolate.

Then off we started again into the night. It was getting harder and harder to keep awake ... We went churning along, our voices vainly chipping at the darkness, at sleep itself ...

'So what do you think about?'

'Well ... ummm ...'

'Come along now, girls, do your job – don't let me fall asleep.'

'Well, what do you think the country ought to do?'

'I don't know, I don't have time to think about it, I work such long hours. All I like is to do a bit of gardening when I've got time – my wife keeps the garden going, but I do a bit when I can – you work funny hours driving these things – you work without a break, and then you've got a fortnight off. You don't get weekends off. Middlesex, that's where I live. Always lived there. If I had to move, for choice I'd go to Devon. I like the climate there.

'I love Scotland, but I've always lived in the south.'

I jammed Tiger in the ribs to wake her up, and she came to and they started talking about Scotland.

About half-past four he pulled up at another café, said, 'Right – I'm turning off here – you go and get me some cigarettes, I'm going to try and get you a lift into Liverpool.' We bought cigarettes and made a parcel of them and crisps and boiled sweets and a copy of *Young Guard*, and he came back.

'Okay, girls. Colin – over there – he'll take you into the city, you'll be alright with him. He's not ready to leave yet – he'll come and get you. Think about me – I'll still be driving when you're in your meeting.' Yawning, we went to the door and waved him out of sight, down the murky dawn-filled highway.

We arrived in Liverpool city centre about half-past five. The driver let us out near the Ladies, which he said opened early, so to wait around. We started to get freezing, after being in lorries, but the Ladies opened about six – or maybe half-past – and the attendant let us settle down for a couple of hours' welcome sleep on the benches inside. She woke us at eight, because it would start to get busy then. Having had a sleep, we were quite good friends, and after we had a wash and did our hair and put on eyeshadow, we went off to look for breakfast. We had quite a nice time – Tiger was full of affability. We went in the British Home Stores and C&A, and tried on their hats, fooling around. It was a pity we hadn't time to see the big ships.

Once we reached the venue for the meeting, we split up and kept away from one another until the next day.

In the room the air was thick with quarrel; everybody knew it, everybody waited for it, that's why everybody had come.

In the evening I got drunk, wandered away from the so-called 'Social', where rows continued to proliferate ('You're riding on our backs, you bastards . . .' 'You came here with your position already fixed . . .' 'Don't be naive, comrade, everybody already has a position on that question . . .')

I wandered away, down a dark side street, arguments and blaring music thumping away from nearby. I fell half into a front garden, and lay there, wondering what to do next. The state-cap I was keen on hadn't turned up, none of the people whose views coincided with mine had turned up either, I didn't know where I was going to be sleeping and wasn't sure I wanted to find out. A group of people turned the corner. They were state-caps.

'Look, it's Squeaks from Derby. Hello, Squeaks.'

'My name isn't Squeaks,' I said, squeakily resentful.

'Well, what are you doing on the floor?'

'I fell over. I'm not in anybody's caucus.'

'Well, you'd better come with us. You can't stay here all night.' Their kindly imperial tones rang out through the Liverpool streets.

'I didn't vote the same way as you over that headline,' I said. This was meant to sound warning but it came out squeaky. They exchanged amused looks – they were so civilised they didn't care whether you voted with them or not, the mere fact that you'd voted against them on the crucial issue of the meeting wasn't about to ruffle them, they were far too self-possessed.

Tiger and I met up again early on Sunday afternoon, to hitch back home. It was far harder to avoid talking about the meeting now that it had happened. As soon as our driver went off to the Gents: 'I stayed at Leon Jameson's,' said Tiger with a smug little smile.

Immediately I felt quite piqued – Leon Johnson was a musician who tied his trousers up with a big piece of string. Then I remembered where I had stayed, and felt better. 'Well, I stayed with some state-caps,' I said, confident that this would be like a red rag to a bull, 'and they were very nice. They gave me a cooked breakfast – sausages, bacon and tomatoes.'

'Didn't you vote the same way as we did, comrade?' said Tiger, to get her own back.

I flushed, and said, 'I don't think we voted the same way on many things.'

'No, not on many things. But I did notice you voted with us on one issue,' she pointed out cattily.

After that, we set to. 'We're pulling out,' said Tiger. 'We're not prepared to work for a paper that would run a headline like that.'

'Where will you go? What other paper is there?'

'We don't have to go anywhere. We can stay where we are. Because when we pull out, the Liverpool people will pull out, and sections all over the country.'

'Then everybody will be back to square one. We might just as well pass a resolution asking the Labour Party to restore Youth Sections. We ought to back the paper as it's coming under attack from the Party apparatus, and you lot are pulling the rug from under it.'

'Listen, comrade, that headline was a fucking dis-grace,' said Tiger in her rolling gritty Glaswegian.

'Yes, I know it was a fucking disgrace but I don't think they'll run it again, after all the row there's been. Do you honestly think they'll do it again?'

Tiger laughed and stubbed out her cigarette. 'Yes, I do.'

Anxious to be out of the bedsit, I washed and dressed and left in good time in the mornings. Early shifts were no problem for me now, I took a leisurely stroll along Friargate, under the trees. After the wide Georgian terraces the road sloped downwards and into town past Cheapside and the dumpy little church of St Werburgh, built on the site of the first settlement, and its Victorian addition. In the early morning the streets were still, only newsagents were open.

The town had grown up in a valley, around the river. Nothing was marked on any map, until the Romans arrived. Rykneild Way reached our part of the world in the first century, in its march northwards. The Romans left, the Saxons arrived, the Danes made sporadic attacks. The land here was part of Mercia and a buffer zone between the Danelaw and the lands of Alfred the Great.

The past is the past but it's all around us. The town streets, built over the river, the piecemeal patchwork of buildings – our town, it's a real kind of place. Dull, but real. There are a few buildings left from Stuart and Georgian times; the odd Roman coin turned over in gardens near Chester Green. But little material is left from the past.

Charles Edward Stuart rode south with an army to conquer Britain, but changed his mind when he got to our town. Well, actually, the banks shut early when they heard he was coming. The exigencies of commerce have always prevailed here without sentimentality. Even the town's patron saint was dug up and tipped out of his church, to make way for a motorway.

In the War, when the German bombers came over, a magic mist formed over the valley, so the crews had no idea where they were. Down below, people in houses and offices and shops closed the curtains and tasted the tar in their mouths and noses, smelled it hanging in their hair and clothes. On each street corner the barrels of pitch were lit, sending up clouds of disguising fog, whilst Rolls-Royce worked twenty-four hours a day, turning out fighter planes.

We had a big row at the Branch round about this time. Ordinarily, heated rows were in the distant past, along with jockeying to take over positions and aligning to defeat other people's resolutions. We got on well with one another, we mulled over the week's events and when we passed resolutions we reached general agreement first. Of course this is much easier to do when there are only five or six people. Although David was more involved with the adult party than the rest of us were, Richard's main loyalties were to CND, and Fiddle wasn't even a member, still – we got on well.

We were all enthused by the Cuban revolution, Fiddle's talks on it were very popular, and three of us went once a month to a boring Co-op meeting to try to pass a resolution about the Co-op buying Algerian and Cuban goods. Che Guevara was immensely popular with the boys – he was more of a boy's taste; I always preferred Fidel, who had to make the Revoluton work afterwards. When I came to read Che's reminiscences of the revolutionary war it turned me off completely when they slaughter the wonderful horse and eat it. A great stain of disappointment spread through me, I reread it to make sure, and then closed the book, wrapped it in a bag so it wasn't visible.

A few days later I handed it back to Fiddle. 'You can keep it,' he said.

'I don't want it.'

Then we had a row. It started because he could scarcely believe what he was hearing.

'They were hungry, and they killed horses to live when they were in the Sierra Maestra,' he said, attempting to accommodate himself to this new twist of feeling in his listeners.

'I'm not taking about the Sierra Maestra, I'm talking about this particular horse . . .'

'You mean,' said David, just the right side of sarcastic, a smile slowly spreading as he exchanged looks with the others, 'it's alright to kill the ordinary horses but not this particular one . . .'

'No, I don't mean that.' If Irene had been here she would have supported me, and I turned to Edna. She and Graham were looking glum, they didn't like rows. Teddy boys had been very discriminated against in the '50s and above their wide shoulders they often had a sad expression, as though they shouldered some ancient unfair disadvantage. They stopped wearing full drape, but still wore the wide shoulders and d.a. hair, to let everybody know that underneath they were still faithful teddy lads.

'Look,' said Richard, blinking and trying to insert reason into the proceedings, 'We mustn't be too squeamish. I agree it isn't pleasant but we aren't in that position and they did what they thought was necessary . . .'

'If Che had said – we were desperately hungry, we killed the horse – but he doesn't say it like that, he gloats.'

'How can you be so soft, when they risked their lives and many lost their lives, to make a revolution for the Cuban people?' demanded Fiddle.

Rick's friend Peter was bent over the book, turning its pages purposefully. Edna said, 'Well, I think it's horrible.' Graham still looked sad.

'When the Revolution reaches Derby, are we going to smash all the beautiful china?'

'We must be careful here, we mustn't impose our ideas and prejudices on other people,' said Richard. 'Cuba is basically a Spanish culture and they have very different ideas about animals.'

Fiddle broke in impatiently. 'What are you talking about? All the dogs and cats in this country eat horse. Look here – we've always said, haven't we, that we wouldn't sit safe over here nit-picking at other people's revolutions? And now you come out with this.'

'Che himself says it was a magnificent animal and he thought it amusing to feed its unknowing rider with its flesh. Che shouldn't have killed that wonderful horse, he should have put it at the service of the Revolution . . .'

'I can't believe I'm hearing this,' Fiddle said furiously. 'Okay – we've all got our handkerchiefs out for the horse – none of us like it – but what you're saying is objectively counter-revolutionary, whatever your intentions.'

'Oh shut up – it was a sly thing to do . . .'

'Come on,' said Edna to Graham, 'we're going' – they started hurriedly buttoning up.

'I'm sorry about the horse,' Graham said, but he meant really that he was sorry the world was such a rotten place. 'What about Justice for the poor of the Americas – do you think it exists? Do you think it isn't as important as a horse?'

'Well, I'm going, I'm not stopping here.' I slammed out and hurried away up the dark street.

That night I fell asleep quickly and dreamed. I was in the dark deserted town streets. Behind closed glass doors and windows all was dark. But when I peered close up to the glass, it was bright inside, ladies and gentlemen were drinking coffee, they had powdered hair and hand-painted fichued gowns and knee-breeches. They were probably china. I ran away quickly in case they made me go in. After that, I turned a corner and had a big row with somebody, but it was so dark I wasn't sure who it was. Then a noise came thundering through the streets, nearer and nearer came a great horse, moving like a lamp holding all brightness in the dark. Its massive feet, its mane floating – it could never be caught, nothing could touch it, nothing could stop it, it had already been slain and now it was invincible.

SPRING

At the Branch we discussed the imminent proscription of *Young Guard*. The meeting broke up early. Afterwards I took off down the dark main road into town alone. The air was clear and fresh, almost warm. At the funeral parlour there was an angled mirror in which I had used every morning to peer at myself on the way to school. Well, I was walking in the opposite direction now, and I hesitated, looking back at the murky glass, full of night now and my face dim and indistinguishable. Behind, some distance away, a male in a white shirt was walking rapidly in the darkness. I thought it might be Richard's friend Peter, but couldn't be sure. I hoped it was him, because I liked him. Walking on, I looked back again, but still couldn't be sure, so slowed my steps for a while, and turned again. He was catching up, so I waited.

'What are you running away for? I'm not going to rape you,' he said rudely.

'I never said you were,' I replied huffily. 'I wasn't sure it was you, my eyes don't work properly and

I didn't want to just *wave*.' We moved downhill into the town.

Young Guard folded, its demise not caused by the threatened proscription, but a spontaneous internal combustion in the form of a faction fight on the editorial board. The town and everyday life were dulled and altered for me now that the hopes bound into the paper had come to nothing. If we couldn't even sustain a paper, what chance was there for the ideas in it, or for a revolution? Yet the intense disappointment was mixed up with relief. The year stretched ahead, free of selling and of the intricacies of book-keeping. The relief reminded me of the time when, at the end of a school summer holiday, my mother had thrown away the ginger-beer plant that yielded pints of liquid but had to be fed relentlessly with ginger and sugar and its weekly offspring decanted into jamjars and palmed off on to friends. A wonderful opportunity lost and it was all somebody else's fault.

'The paper's folded,' I told Chris. 'I've got batches and batches of it – some to send out, four and ninepence-worth to sell myself.'

'Four and nine – what a coincidence – exactly the price of a vodka and lime, fruit.'

'Yes – *one* vodka and lime.'

'We can toss for it,' she suggested happily.

'We don't need to do that – I don't see why you should get a vodka and lime off the backs of the suffering masses.'

'You can't be serious, Sylvie – I *am* one of the suffering masses – all those subscribers I'm constantly nice to, I work my fingers to the bone in the service of the GPO: I broke a fingernail this morning.'

'Okay – if you sell the papers, you can keep the money.' Chris was pleased about this arrangement, she could easily sell them and it's a novelty, to sell a paper once. Chris examined the front-page headline with puzzled semi-interest and read out wonderingly, '"*Young Guard* says Don't leave the Labour Party – make them throw you out."'

In the afternoon Janet and Gaily asked if I had any more papers they could sell.

Ronni bought a new rucksack and she and Val Pepper went hitch-hiking at weekends, all over Derbyshire, in their stout boots and red nail polish.

Miss Blair, always every hair in place, had an extra gloss. The Spring Speech Festivals had started and she was either adjudicating, or worrying over her best pupils' performances. Her hair in a long, brunette page-boy, she wore her favourite crimson – a gown of full rich cramoisie.

I went off in a noisy coach to a Trafalgar Square demo ... Afterwards I stayed with Nessie and Tony, who were in the Committee of a Hundred. Tony was a solicitor who had defended Nessie from a charge of obstruction and then married her. Nessie made cauliflower cheese coloured pink with beetroot, and she said it was healthy to have sex, it did you good, that the Marie Stopes Clinic fitted caps on females whether they were married or not, and that dutch-caps were safer than sheaths.

I reported back to the Branch on everything

that had happened, on the stone lions and gushing water, on the rip-off ice-creams for a pound, the police charges on horseback, the plot of *Hiroshima Mon Amour* which we had seen the next afternoon at the Academy Cinema, and what Nessie had said about the direness of sheaths.

'Oh I know,' agreed Peter enthusiastically. 'Les, our foreman, he doesn't like sheaths either. He said wearing them is like trying to have a bath with your boots on.' I felt it was my duty to inform them of all this extra information – you had to share knowledge, because knowledge is power.

It was late spring, I was on a four o'clock shift, the sun was on the unfurling ash leaves along Friargate, switchboard operators tip-tapped from the Exchange, scholars padded home on thick-soled plimsolls.

Peter was in the Gainsborough, sitting over a book and a cup of coffee, books spilling from his satchel on the chair.

'Can I see this?' Hesitant, I touched his book almost shyly, as though it had been a secret place in his body.

'Metaphysicals,' he said, pushing it in my direction. The book was small and pencilled on and its spine was broken, and it fell open at 'The Definition of Love'. I read silently and slowly and I liked it very much. 'Do you really like that?' He smiled, and I nodded. 'I can't decide,' he said, 'whether it isn't surreptitiously romantic – all that stuff about Fate.'

'Rick doesn't believe in Fate,' I said. 'He thinks Fate is awful.'

'You'll like this one,' he said enthusiastically. 'You'll approve of it.' And he flipped through the pages and handed me the open book. I slipped out of my shoes and put my feet on the rung of his chair and began to read 'Had we but World enough and Time . . .' Centuries old, it was new to us.

Peter was tall and big and I felt giddy being near him. He looked strong and fresh, and sweet as a nut, his shirt open at the neck in the best proletarian style, he had cropped luxuriant hair and simple straightforward manners.

'Rick says Plato's heaven is where naked minds contemplate the eternal.'

Peter laughed. 'Do you care about the eternal?'

'Yes, I think so.'

'Do you really?' He smiled at me and I had an intense feeling I hadn't the faintest idea what I was talking about.

'Well. I'm not sure what it is.'

'Neither am I.'

We grinned at one another, the bubbles exploded in the coffee, the waitresses hurried about the crowded room in their snowflaky aprons. Near the polished wood stairs were the sacks of coffee beans, at the back of the counter was the mirror which cast all back, as it had from the beginning of our world.

I handed him the copy of *The Second Sex* that Fiddle had given me.

179

'Thanks. I'll read it quickly, I'm not spending my last holiday reading books.'

After their exams finished Rick started part-time tutoring, and Peter went from just Saturdays to working all week on the building site.

'Pete isn't a revolutionary, you know. Not really. He's Labour, that's all,' said Rick critically.

'So?'

'Well, I'm just pointing it out.'

Rick had a girlfriend now, she was called Britt, she didn't wear tight skirts and she was an art student. He mentioned her quite a lot, and he left Branch meetings early to meet her. 'Oh God – are you still seeing that stupid bloody Pre-Raphaelite?' said Peter. Everybody froze in horror. It sounded like a terrible new swear word.

Rick got very huffy. 'Yes. I am. If it's any of your business.'

Love and Liberty were doing fine but dear me, the Friendship was getting a little vinegary.

'What's a Pre-Raphaelite?' I asked Ronni.

'Hmmm. How do you spell it, Sylvia?'

'Haven't the faintest idea.'

'Well I'm Fault Telephonist this afternoon, I'll ask on the Button.'

At three o'clock the glass light on each board glowed, and round the Switchroom every operator pressed their Button, to hear 'Does anybody know what a Pre-Raphaelite is? Does anybody know what a Pre-Raphaelite is? Does . . .'

Peter . . . I saw the light in his dark eyes and the pulse jump in his neck and watched him talk hardly hearing a word now. Under a white shirt his body was dark and gold, from working on site all day. I walked home with a gold dark boy.

After the union meeting I rushed over to the Spotted Horse, to meet Peter. 'We've decided to vote in favour of a strike,' I said excitedly. 'Come on – let's go somewhere else.'

Peter was drinking up when Chris and Susan and the others came in. '*Hi* – you're not *going* . . .?' So we stayed for one drink, all of us excited. I felt wonderfully happy, Susan was at her gayest, Chris was bubbling with laughter, Peter was smiling and just enough mesmerised by how pretty and how strong we were, to be voting to strike.

'Let's go now,' I whispered to him, and he smiled at me and opened both palms into the air to indicate complaisance.

'Did you like the others? Which one of them did you like best?'

He looked put out at this, and said, 'Which one do you suggest?'

'I don't specially want you to like any of them. I want you to like me.'

We left, the world was at its best, the evening had just begun and the town was alive with lights and voices as we walked down St James's Street.

'What's the matter with you?' he said. We were crossing the street and it was fairly teeming with people but I didn't care, I was in that sort of mood.

'Okay,' I said, in a sudden fury arriving out of nowhere. 'If we had world enough and time – do you want me to drop my drawers now and we can have sexual intercourse right here?'

He looked straight back at me with full brown eyes which plainly said what the hell are you doing? and then he answered, in a voice indignant and robust and just as loud, 'No I don't want to have "sexual intercourse"' – he decorated the words with sarcastic inverted commas – 'with you right here. We've never even kissed, for God's sake.'

We strolled on, past the gawpers. His walk was a sort of stolid plodding that looked slow but was actually rapid, because of his size. I asked him whether this was a complaint or an attempt to dissociate himself from me. 'It's neither. It's a statement of fact.' I was silent. Then I said I was going home. He walked with me to the beginning of the main road. When I looked round he was watching me go. He looked despondent, confused, and of all the things in the world, I most wanted to turn back and kiss him. But there was next week, and the week after that, and the week after that – there was all summer before he went away, and it was going to be great. Wanting it too much, I waved goodbye, full of hope. He nodded back disconsolately and pushed himself away from the wall and turned back towards town.

There had been hours and hours more for us I wanted him to talk to me, about everything about poems, and of when he was a little boy and of how the world should be and how the world was. But it would have been too much like everything I really wanted. He thought I wa strong and would always know what to do. He takes me completely seriously, I thought. As well as novel and attractive, this was alarming. The last three years he had been at school, I'd been at work, and suddenly I felt utterly exhausted. The relentless compulsion we had at work to be blithe and to make light of things was also exhausting. It kept us afloat yet it was starting to seem bitter. I was eighteen; Joy at eighteen was full of me, and the idea of this exhausted me too, as though nothing could ever happen, as though it had already happened before.

The day gradually faded from the room and I lay there, not drawing the curtains or making a drink. Then suddenly thirsty, I poured water into a mug – I should have put the kettle on ages ago for a hot drink. Half-thinking, I took tablets from my handbag and took a couple, slowly, with the water. It was like all the energy had fizzed away and the world had gone flat; nothing would happen, this silence in the room would go on and on, the mirror on the dressing-table would reflect nothing; the sudden babble of voices in the distance outside would be saying nothing, over and over, pointlessly. The tablets were round and shiny orange, like beads, and I took them one by one, one by one. Like a catholic telling the rosary, bead after bead after bead. Nothing happened, but something would happen soon – only one little tablet more – or perhaps the next one . . . a quantitative change to a qualitative change . . . Detached, only even half-interested, I waited for something to happen. Perhaps . . .

There was a thumping on the door. Then a voice. 'Hey – come on, Dormouse, wake up.' Dizzily I swung from the bed and opened the door.

It was Susan. 'Hi – have you got a shilling? Hey – are you alright? – you look quite peculiar – your eyes have gone black.'

'I've just taken lots of tablets,' I said, swaying and feeling stupid.

'You'd better have black coffee or something – I'll make some.'

'It takes about an hour for that thing to get hot.'

'Come on then, you'd better come to mine. Oh, have you got a shilling?'

'It's okay,' she said later, handing me about the eighth mug of coffee. 'You can do the same for me when I take my overdose.' She wandered around her small room with its sloping ceiling, her eyes shining. 'I come alive at night. I can't sleep,' she said, going over to the window.

He was there on Wednesday. The meeting didn't have much to discuss – or perhaps it did? – and we were soon alone, walking in the darkness towards town.

'I'd got a raging headache last week and it made me ratty. I'm sorry.' He looked down at me and grinned.

'Let's walk by the station and the canal. I like it there, you can hear the trains as they pass.'

We wandered along the road away from the town, making for Drum Hill, which was a few miles away. 'My father used to come here when he was in the Scouts as a boy. And my uncle. And in the summers all the boys in our street used to disappear suddenly, and that's where they'd gone.'

He laughed. 'So did I. My brother still comes to camp here. It's over the other side of the hill, though.'

'Ann's granny used to come here to an old fair when she was a girl – Shuttlecock Fair – every spring. They always used to walk home singing "I'll cling to you, just like the ivy on the old garden wall".' We laughed. 'They don't hold the fair any more, there's nothing left of it now except hearsay.'

As we walked, cars sped past smoothly on the wide main road, disappearing into the far silence. We walked on, treading this land where the past disintegrates under your feet. We reached the trees, an earthy smell rising from between them.

'Gosh, I'm exhausted, the backs of my legs ache . . .' In the air our voices left trails of moisture, and trees sighed and breathed all about.

Through the dark came his voice, touching me all over, bringing me alive. 'It's warm.'

'Yes.'

He touched me lightly and we were together, I reached for him fervently and he caught all my complaisance between his hands. Then in the warm night my teeth were chattering.

'Please . . .'

'What is it? Why are you shaking?'

'Please – oh please don't let me have a baby.'

'You mean,' he laughed softly into the darkness, 'all that stuff about Marie Stopes . . .?'

I broke away from him and said indignantly, 'Well, I am in favour of it, because of . . . of personal liberty and anyway, what about the population problem?'

He clapped a soft hand over my mouth and pulled me to him and kissed me lots and lots, not on the mouth but like children kiss at parties. All around us black leaves shaking and beyond his head I could see stars throbbing like heartbeats.

'Yes?'

'Yes.'

Yes Yes YES, to everything. We lay down and kissed quietly, he held my hand and then he blasted straight into me and there was a great warm pain that I wanted and had feared.

In the lively night I lay watching him sleep, trying to make out his features in the darkness. I was too excited for sleep, every pore in my body was alive and zinging. Through the trees came small noises of creatures, rabbits, a flutter and squawk of a bird in the crackling quilt of ferns putrefying from last year, and Time rushed past beating its wings. I was in that world now where the moment ripens the moment and all that belongs to it, from bud to flower to seed relentlessly.

I was dying to wake him up, but his slumber was precious and trusting. Then in the grey early light his eyelashes flickered and he reached for me.

'Again?'

'Mmmmm.'

This time he was hurt too. 'Christ!' He ripped suddenly out of me and held himself and tried to smile.

'What is it?' I whispered.

'Oh. I expect I'll live,' he smiled mockingly. And then he put his big warm arms around me and I fell asleep.

SWITCHBOARD
OPERATORS II

The town and daily working life had come to seem flat. Rick and Peter had left for university. Many of the telegraph-boys had turned twenty-one and left. Bob Greenhough became a bus-conductor, Jim joined the RAF, Ron passed his exams and got a good job in industry. Only Noddy was left out of our class, to put on his postman's uniform. Fiddle too had thrown up his job rather than give up his motorbike. Soon afterwards, he bought his own motorbike and took off on it to the continent.

Gaily was disappointed, although nobody could understand why, because Fiddle had always said marriage was a function of bourgeois society, made necessary by private property relations, and Gaily's main ardent hope was to marry.

Ronni had met somebody whilst hiking, and got engaged. I bumped into her in Ranby's, in a crush of white net, trying wedding dresses on again.

'What do you think?'

'Looks lovely,' I said, unable to get too enthusiastic because I didn't think for one minute she would be wearing it.

'Mike wants a traditional wedding, but I don't know ... I fancy a sheath dress and white gladioli at the Registry Office ...' Her voice trailed off vaguely, as her eyes alighted on yet another wedding veil.

In the Retiring Room Gaily was gloomy because Fiddle had gone, and Susan was laid low, because Bill had left her for somebody else.

'Never mind, fruitdrop. He's not worth the agony, you know.'

'Well, Susie, you could always do-a-Flossie.'

Doing-a-Flossie was named after an operator who, back in the time when Edwardian mists swirled about the first telephone exchanges and men caught electrical impulses like fairies from the air, had got her revenge on a married lover who left her by ringing his wife and connecting her to the conversation he was having with his new girlfriend.

Susan tipped her head on one side and asked of the air, 'Would I stoop that low, I ask myself?'

'You might, fruit.'

Susan rearranged this sentence and batted it back detachedly. 'Yes, fruit, I might.'

'And you'd be out on your ear if you did, madam. It's not exactly part of the Friendly Telephone service, is it? I don't think it was quite what Mr Marples had in mind,' said Noreen.

Susan laughed joylessly. 'Huh – that's all I need – to lose my job as well.'

The Branch – all four of us – got a card postmarked Paris: 'Arrived Thursday. Going to the Sorbonne tomorrow to hear Krivine. Bike broke down on motorway. Don't forget Co-op meeting. Venceremos, Fiddle.'

Val had been seen out with Mr Cox, after she and her boyfriend had split up. 'Just think – they'll be able to have lots of lovely rows,' said Ann.

Just before we had left College, Mr Cox had come into the classroom, grinning.

'Well. I've joined.' He smacked his hands together.

'Joined?' we echoed.

'Yes. I've joined.' He opened his corduroy jacket and pulled something from the inner pocket. It was a small card with the logo of a crossed shovel and pen and words about securing for the workers by hand or by brain the full fruits of their industry.

'What a fine example of the Elenchus,' Rick had said, his eyes sparkling blue with delight on being told of it. The Elenchus – there ought to be more of it.

Now that Rick and Peter had gone, life seemed so dull. Dr Laurence suggested I take GCEs. 'I can't, it's too late.'

'Oh, it's never too late. When I was a young man I had to postpone my studies and serve in the forces, because we were at war. I did my medical training late, after I came out of the RAF. You're still in your teens and you're talking as though your life is nearly over.'

In a way, I felt as though it was, and if it wasn't then it would be just too hard to sustain for years and years.

In the autumn I went to sign on for English at

evening class. It proved more difficult than I had expected. The Tech was crowded with people, and I asked a man who looked like a teacher where to enrol.

'Is it English for Typists?' he responded.

'No, it's just English.'

He gave me directions, I spent ages pushing my way through milling crowds, and when I found the classroom and waited in the queue, it turned out to be English for Typists. At the signing desk they gave me some more directions, and I took off again into the crowds, and got lost; the classroom I ended up in had no signing for English. I turned away, and asked a teacher just on his way in, 'Excuse me, where can I sign on for English, please?'

He said kindly, 'Is it English for Nurses?'

This made me smile, I like nurses and would like to have done nursing if I hadn't been at the Exchange. I smiled probably rather happily but I definitely said no, and I was listening to myself this time. 'No. Just English.'

He gave me directions, and when I got there, it turned out to be English for Nurses.

By this time I was getting rattled, the crowds were thinning, my feet were killing me because I'd been to so many classrooms, and this was the last night to enrol.

'Excuse me.' I spoke slowly so there was no reason for him not to understand. 'Could you please tell me where to sign on for English? Just English. Not English for Nurses and not English for Typists. Plain English.'

He smiled benevolently and said, 'It's alright, don't worry, I know what you want. It's English for Foreigners, isn't it?'

I stopped listening to him and walked away, nearly in tears with frustration, when a yell came across the courtyard – 'Hey, Dormouse.'

It was Julie Jones and Mavis and a bunch of the others from the Exchange. 'I can't stop, I'm looking for English to sign on, and it will be too late soon.'

'That's alright – that's what we've all come for, it's this way – you can come with us.'

So I tagged along and it was quite simple. Afterwards, I went over the contents of the exchanges in my head, and wondered why my no hadn't registered; the teachers I spoke to behaved as though it hadn't been uttered.

Ronni and Val's leave-of-absence came through, and Ronni broke her engagement and they took off to hitch-hike through Italy for six months.

The longer you stayed at the Exchange, the nearer loomed the figure of the Bride. It was all around, no tea-break was complete without girls talking of their coming weddings, planning the dress, recalling other girls as brides, showing round photographs.

To stay at the Exchange past the mid-twenties brought you closer to the figure of the Supervisor, and behind it loomed the Spinster. Some of the supervisors, like Miss Armitage, lived in the shelter of the notion of a great service, which enriched their working lives. Miss Armitage went hospital visiting, she packed her basket with goodies and treats for her patients, and on Wednesday nights she hurried off to her Brownie pack, St Werburga's Patrol. She showed her little girls, their eyes shining, how to cook and tie knots and recognise flags, and afterwards they sang 'Westering Home' in the dancing firelight. The Divisional Supervisor was little Miss Mills, who sat at her desk in the afternoons, monitoring the switchboard operators, making sure we were giving a proper service. You never knew if she was listening in to you. She scurried round, faffing – to use a word in vogue then among the switchboard operators – and it did seem to describe a flurry of ruffled feathers and panic.

Apart from Mrs Royle, who was everybody's favourite supervisor, I couldn't see the point of the married ones, who didn't have children or Brownie packs. In the Supervisors' Staffroom, where she was known as Frankie, Mrs Francis was regarded as a jolly blonde, but in the Switchroom she was often suppressing a yawn. And Mrs Lord, with great fatigue examining her stocking seams. They gave out an aura of ennui. Miss Mills and Miss Armitage, faffing and panicking, and little hard-drinking Miss Jones, at least imparted a feeling that what you did mattered. We could only really conjecture what the supervisors were like. Being older, they were probably much more interesting than we were. But we didn't think so, and we didn't see them as they were. The figure of the Spinster, when you turn the lights on and examine it at close quarters, there isn't much to it, it's a sleight of hand, a confidence trick on a grand scale, the shadow thrown by the Bride.

'Marriage damages your brain. Look at Miss Arden.'

'Gosh, yes.'

Miss Arden was the Travelling Supervisor. She would ring in and say briskly, 'This is the Travelling Supervisor here,' and you had to connect her instantly and without charge. Seldom seen, she travelled about putting switchboards aright, showing firms how to operate them correctly and to their maximum advantage, and checking faults; advising on purchases most suitable to their needs. Occasionally she would sweep into the Exchange, very tall in tweed cloak and matching pencil skirt, and blonde bobbed hair, and the whisper went around the boards, 'Miss Arden' 'Miss Arden' 'Miss Arden', and all the operators turned to see.

Then there were the Acting Supervisors, Fanny and company. Pale, soft-voiced Mercia, who wore jabots and lace bits; Moira, with the sergeant-major manner and face pushed truculently into her neck as she told you off; Hildegard, blonde and chain-smoking; she wed a British soldier in 1945; the Elton sisters, Anne and Emmy, who wore makeup like models and tailored clothes — they were good old-fashioned girls, they wanted to have a good time and then marry rich husbands. And mixed in with the career women and the disappointed in love and the gold-diggers were the dolly-daydreams, who were just never decisive enough for marriage or commitment, they never seemed to wake up, went through each day in a dream, and Time crept up and overtook them and then they were supervisors.

Chris said, 'You know, I've never felt old enough to be a Girl Guide.'

'I know what you mean, fruit. I never recovered from being a Brownie.'

'What – you mean all those knots you had to tie – it permanently weakened you?'

'You can scoff – being a Brownie can be quite exhausting.'

As a child, I'd been to several Brownie packs. They showed you how to lay tables and recognise flags, Brown Owl examined your hair and fingernails to make sure they were clean, and you had to try to do a Good Deed every day. Then I found this really good pack. It was further away but more wild, they had pow-wows and screamed more. And at the end of the evening the lights went out and we turned into animals. The firelight cracked and lapped over us and Brown Owl issued her commands.

'Now, Brownies – you are all going to turn into BEARS, and I want to hear you growl – louder. Louder. No, Jennifer, you're a bear and bears don't moo . . . *Now* you are all going to turn into . . . MICE – can I hear you squeak?'

'Weet weet weet, weet weet weet . . .'

'And now you are . . . LIONS.'

The blood raced in our veins, the darkness filled with roaring, as we called up the jungle.

Janet and Rita had met two boys at the Locarno. They were called Ray and Dek, and the girls were very taken with them. They sat in the Retiring Room talking about them, and making plans to go out as a foursome.

'Aaaaah,' said Janet, 'you should see Dek's letters, they're so sweet, he can't spell for toffee,' she said fondly.

Monday night was Locarno night. After the weekend everybody was short of money, but not yet down to pennies. The Locarno entrance fee was halved on Monday evenings, so that was when we went.

There were three floors – the ground floor, where the dance floor was and the orchestra. Mondays, being half-price, it was records. The balcony was upstairs, where people sat at tables with drinks, looking down at the dancers. Ranged up the wide staircase were waiting boys, watching you as you passed, all up the stairs and leaning over the balustrade, their eyes watched as you made your way to the Powder Room in a little group.

The sumptuous Powder Room seemed like half an acre of pink tiling and soft carpet and mirrors, and constant scented air-conditioning. There was an attendant, and urns of flowers, and the perfume-dispensers were unlike the dispensers in the town conveniences, which were rackety and empty, except for Tweed. The Locarno dispensers worked like a dream, there was a queue to put a shilling in, hands cupped to catch Blue Grass and splash it quickly about your hair and throat.

I used to like to go up to the top floor, which on Mondays was usually deserted and resembled somebody's attic, unused tables and chairs stacked together, and an old bar that had been ripped out from downstairs and was obviously in store up here. You could look down on the colourful figures, intersecting like a kaleidoscope, and drop your Coke straw and wonder where it would land. Hanging over the edge of the balcony up here you were almost at a level with the net of balloons that lay there until New Year, when they were allowed to float down on the peal of bells.

Drenched in Pagan, I went with Irene and the petticoats, who always came on Mondays. In fact, you saw most people then. Graham and Edna were sometimes there, and Brenda Boulton, who went on a date with Vince Eager, was usually whirling round in a red dress. You jigged about to the records and faces jigged into vision briefly – faces from school, from work, faces from the chemist's, the railway, Woolworth's, faces last seen years before. 'Hi Sylvia' – 'Hi Dinah' – a wave, a smile, and the dancing carried them away again, back into the childhood past.

When everyone was exhausted from jiving, they put on a slow smoochy one, the lights were dimmed and you slid into your partner's arms, whoever they were. At the end of the evening 'Save the Last Dance for Me' echoed about the near-empty building as girls looked for dropped bags and lone earrings under chairs.

A crowd was sitting round a table, Janet and Rita and their new boyfriends, the mysterious Ray and Dek. They turned out to be Raymond Shipham and Derek Foss, last seen at the Infants. The teacher had always said their names as one – 'Raymond Shipham-and-Derek Foss – Come here/Stop that/Stay behind/I shall tell your mothers . . .' They were double-trouble. They played Rosy Apples on the way home from school, and pulled the girls' pigtails. And one day – the first time the class had PT, dressed in plimsolls and knickers and T-shirts. Everybody got very wild at this new experience. On the way out of school I walked with spinning head, staring at my feet – there seemed to be something the matter with them. It must have happened during PT. Slowly I moved each step, trying to puzzle out what had gone wrong. Suddenly a shower of droplets hit them and I stopped dead still, looked up and saw Raymond Shipham-and-Derek Foss, they had their little winkies out and were spraying each other and anybody else around, gleefully they bellowed laughter about the playground.

'Come along, away from those two naughty boys,' called my mother, at the school gates.

'Something's happened to my feet,' I said.

She looked down and laughed. 'You've put your shoes back on the wrong feet.'

Anyway, these were Dek and Ray, now the enamoured of Janet and Rita. They sat at a table. Ray was the awful one, he cracked jokes and teased Rita practically the whole time. Dek was the strong, silent one. I don't think I've ever heard his voice, even though we went to school together, and then he was Janet's husband. Probably we'll bump into each other in the old folks' home and we might manage a couple of sentences then, when we're old and doddery. After I left the Exchange I lost touch with Chris and Janet, but then bumped into Janet in Sainsbury's and she said, 'Come to Dek's birthday party, he doesn't want one but he's having one anyway.' Next time I saw her, they were divorced. We passed in the street one time and looked at each other curiously. I was thinking: I was a Mixed Infant with him, what's he doing round here? and he was glaring at me and obviously thinking: 'I was a Mixed Infant with her, what's she doing round here?', because it was a red-light street. I was recovering from a love affair, my life was in tatters and it was a cheap place to live. He must have been there because he and Janet were divorced; she had the house and the children so maybe he had gone to live where it was cheap too.

Pamela Heath got drunk in the Spotted Horse after a union meeting, and when everybody wanted to go home, they called a taxi and bundled her into it, and gave the driver her address. When the taxi arrived and her husband opened the door, he was mad because she was drunk and he didn't agree with unions anyway and thought she was spending too much time on union matters. He left her in the taxi, paid the driver and told him to take her back to the GPO. Next morning the eight o'clock shift found her asleep on the Exchange steps, and when roused, she couldn't remember what had happened. She splashed her face with cold water in the cloakroom, borrowed a clean blouse from Sal, and went to join the postmen having their breakfasts, before going on to the boards. After work, she moved back to her mother's.

Sitting on the boards, summoning souls, summoning voices, switchboard operators on the outside of other people's dramas. Above us the clock, the same clock face repeated throughout the Switchroom, and in every switchroom in the land. It was suspended sideways on an arc, so we could easily see it in order to register the time on dockets. Before us, a day's work ahead and the board face – the answering field with its play of lights, the strips of lines to dial local exchanges – Alstonefield, Ambergate, Ashbourne, Ashby-de-la-Zouche . . . Belper, Breadsall, Brailsford, Buxton . . . Coalville, Cowers Lane . . . Castle Donington . . . Somerfields – the operators no longer quite Winnie and Alma and company, just voices, disappearing voices . . . Ambergate, where Mr Cox had his farm – somebody else would be connecting him to the Waterworks these days. Above, the lines to distant exchanges and the trunk lines – London Faraday and Nottingham Trunk, where our calls were routed to exchanges all over the country. At our fingertips, the dial to the right, to the left the file of exchanges and their dialling codes – the staid, ordinary ones, and the nutty ones – Knockmedown, St Just-in-Roseland, Westward Ho!, Wantage, Ballymakelligot . . . And the names with the tricksy pronunciations, periodically mentioned in Refresher – Milngavie, Shrewsbury, Wymondham, Alnwick. But sometimes we were instructed to take the more straightforward pronunciation.

'Now,' said Miss Armitage, 'you may often hear local people refer to their exchange as *Uttch*eter. *You* are to pronounce it Yut*tox*eter, as we take the standard BBC pronunciation on this one. Repeat back the number, but leave out the exchange name. You are not to correct subscribers who say Uttcheter, or to repeat it back the way you have been told to say it.'

I should jolly well think not!

'Presumably local people know best how their town is to be pronounced,' put in Joan.

Miss Armitage looked sweet and regretful. 'Yes. I'm afraid it's one of these difficult cases. It tends mostly to be older people who say Uttcheter, so it does seem to be dying out. It is a shame, I agree. But we are instructed by the GPO to take the standard BBC pronunciation in this case. I don't know who makes these decisions . . .'

'Goole is the name I like least,' said Margaret afterwards. 'Little Peover and Chipping Sodbury at least have something about them – but Goole! It makes me think of a wet Monday morning.'

Chris narrowed her eyes with laughter and said West Wittering was her favourite – it made her think of Miss Armitage and Miss Mills dashing about the Switchroom in a panic. Miss Armitage, fragile and unworldly, was a great favourite of both of us.

'Snodland sounds a lovely place,' said newly married Judy. 'A mixture of snogging and the Land of Nod.' Judy, in a billowy lemon dress, was all ready to enjoy herself at a regatta in the afternoon. All week she went about the Exchange binding wounds and dispensing sympathy, but both her parents had died when she was small, and nobody could do anything about that.

'Miss Sands, is Mrs Harlowe's headset still in your locker?' asked Miss Armitage. 'We've looked everywhere for it, and we need it now for someone else.'

Elly had left well over a year ago but her headset was still dangling from a peg in our locker, like something slain and hung up. But I liked it where it was, I didn't feel alone. 'I don't think so.' Miss Armitage went away. Elly and I had never met again, the half-knitted matinée jacket with its dropped stitches was still in a brown paper bag on the locker shelf.

'That's not too bad, fruit,' said Jennifer. 'It will be alright when you've finished it off and put a pink ribbon in.'

Elly had never altered the label showing her maiden name, and I hadn't removed it after she left, so the locker still appeared to belong to Miss E.A. Hurst, Miss S. Sands, Ellaline Alicia, Christine Clare, Jennifer Ann, Ann Rosemary – what were parents doing when they named their young? Ellaline Alicia – their baby disappeared into flowers and a dream of white and the bride curled round in the bride, forever.

As Ronni looked over Verona, at the sun on the pink buildings, on Juliet's crumbling balcony, the teeming city above the catacombs of the Perfect – she thought it strange she was here and how it had all begun with a human call ground from a piece of moving plastic. 'I want to see it all – everything, not just the grand buildings but the countryside and the everyday bits, even the last little geranium in the window of the tiniest house in the littlest cobbled alley,' she said intensely. She surrendered herself to an unknown country, her mind and senses spinning, Ronni the tough, the trendsetter, all washed away.

They sat sipping campari and watching street activity: carried their bits of chiffon to cover hair to show respect whilst visiting village churches; slapped sun-tan oil on each other's backs; they got lost in Venice. Venice in the rain.

They made their way between sloping terraces laid out on a hillside, stopping at the side of a road, where a glass case held a home-made shrine to the Baby, in a wicker cradle decked with frills and ribbons and satin bows. 'Oh Val, oh look – oh isn't it sweet?' said Ronni, her eyes suddenly full of tears at the thought of all the love that had been stitched into the tiny blankets and babyclothes, made to keep Him warm. The girls stood smiling before the cradle, as before a fire that flickered warmth and light, their eyes feasting and joyful. Round the side was written in even biroed letters '*La bella bambina Maria, a destine la madre di Dio*'.

Shocked to the core, they turned unspeaking back to the road. They walked about half a mile, before Ronni said, 'Did you see what it said, Val?'

'Yes,' said Val grimly.

'You know, we really are in a foreign country,'

and Ronni peered about into the shivering olive leaves as though half-expecting some tricky sprite to pounce out of them.

'Come on, let's race to the bottom of the hill and blow away all the cobwebs.' They sped away on their long legs.

As it turned out, although our Branch voted in favour, we didn't go on strike that year. In fact, the UPW didn't strike for the first time until 1971, and then they stayed out for months. It was a long and bitter dispute, which the Union finally lost, just as subsequently many unions lost ground in the 1970s.

In the Retiring Room Susan sat stroking her lashes with mascara, bringing her eyes into relief. 'Have you seen anything of Bill, Susiboots?'

'No, sugar-plum.' She didn't sound bothered, her voice detached, her hand never faltered as she applied colour, and then pursed her lips and blew a kiss like a farewell kiss in the compact mirror. Then she took a white lipstick and carefully obliterated her lips, looking from side to side at herself in the glass after she had finished. Bloodless, uncarnal, all-eyes. As she shut the compact she said, casual and remote, 'I've always wondered – supposing one day you looked into the mirror, and there was nothing there?' A sudden glum silence echoed back at her from the girls round the table.

I lost weight and was starving most of the time

– even the Canteen cabbage had started to seem tantalisingly aromatic.

Late in the year my Aunty Mavis came to see me. She passed a critical eye over the parrots and the cooking arrangements, and asked about the rent. She pinched my arm and said, 'Well, if you stay here much longer there'll be nothing left of you. The best thing you can do is – put all your stuff into carrier-bags, call a taxi, and come to us. I shall charge you the same' – she pointed a warning finger – 'but you'll get your meals as well.'

Aunty Mavis and Uncle Clive lived about three miles out of town, on a pleasant countrified council estate. I was back again in the world of proper meals and decent bedtimes. At night I had to creep in, undress in the bathroom, and steal into bed without putting on the light. If drunk I had to take more care not to fall over. I shared a bedroom with Sharon, who was seven and had monster nosebleeds. She would wake in the middle of the night: 'By dose is bleedig again.'

'Oh gosh' – I would shoot out of bed frantically and hover.

'You'd better get by bubby if you don't dow what to do,' Sharon said reproachfully.

Some weeks Uncle Clive worked nights at Royces, and he probably got more rest in the day anyway, as it was quite noisy at nights, with the nosebleeds and the baby, who rhythmically battered his head against the headboard of his cot, like a charging bull. During school holidays their cousins Ann and Cynthie came, and night-times were even noisier then.

In the week Aunty Mavis cooked and shopped, and made clothes for the children on her sewing-machine; she sat treadling for hours in their large sunny sitting-room. At weekends, they were out doing the garden, and when they had finished they were exhausted, they sent me to their local for a big bottle of cider.

Aunty Mavis insisted on sending my skirts and blue tartan suit to the dry-cleaners regularly. 'I can't afford it!' I yelped out, and it was true.

'Well, you're going to have to afford it, because I'm not having you walking out of my front-door looking as though you've just jumped out of a hedge. I shall stop you a small amount each week – you won't notice it. And I've thrown away that awful coat.'

'What!' It was my favourite marshmallow coat, and I went picking through the dustbin to retrieve it. But she was very bossy. We had quite a few rows.

Rick biked round over his holidays to tell about Oxford.

Now we were no longer at Tech, we were sent relieving in the winter months too. Chris was sent on early duty to Somerfields and, one by one, all the operators rang in to say they had 'flu and weren't coming in. As the flakes spun by outside the window and the discs dropped down on the boards, she realised she was alone. Upstairs Night Irene and her family were prostrate in their beds and the snow fell relentlessly. Aged nineteen, Chris ran Somerfields Exchange all by herself all day.

'What!' said Susan Arnot, aghast. 'A silly little thing like you, in charge of a telephone exchange!'

Chris said feebly, 'Don't remind me, fruit – I could faint every time I think of it.'

'Well, Chrissy, that's marvellous,' I said jealously, 'it's like something in the *Girls' Book of Heroines* – Christine Holds the Fort, like Grace Darling or something. You can do anything if you try.' Chris shot me a particularly withering look. She wasn't really interested in the Dictatorship of the Proletariat, there was no use pretending.

I applied for a transfer to a London exchange, just as Kath had done. She had gone off in a cloud of Coty L'Aimant and smiles and dancing eyelashes, and never been heard of since. 'London's alright,' Flora pronounced darkly, 'as long as you behave yourself.' This sounded really interesting.

Transfers could take a long time to come through, but I was summoned to the presence remarkably speedily. 'The Meringue wants to see you.' I hurried off along the corridor, past the red hanging buckets with FIRE painted on them, past the lift silently sliding up and down, up the stone stairs and into the sudden beehive noise of the Switchroom.

Miss Mills came fussing towards me. 'Miss Sands, Miss Marriott would like to speak to you.' She went hurrying ahead, to conduct me to the desk of the Chief Supervisor.

Dolly was on the telephone, she composed her flutters and motioned gracefully with pink enamelled fingertips for me to sit down . . .

She had summoned me to say that my application for a transfer had been turned down. She had not recommended it. 'I feel that you would be likely to be in moral danger. I don't consider that you are responsible enough, or have any real understanding of the pitfalls that can arise.'

I gulped back disappointment, and when she had finished speaking I said, 'What about Nottingham? Could I have a transfer to Nottingham?' Nottingham was great, I sometimes went at weekends now; the demos there were big and there were parties on 26th July.

The Meringue flickered one of her quick brown toasted looks and said smartly, smoothly, 'You can of course apply. I shall not recommend you for a transfer there. And I may say, Miss Sands, I shall not recommend you for a transfer anywhere.' She launched into a mish-mash of too-much-sick-leave, late-for-duties . . .

'I thought my time-keeping had improved,' I offered deferentially.

'Yes, for the moment. But your conduct is not satisfactory in other respects. What about all these so-called "demonstrations"?'

'But that's in my own time,' I said, quite timidly actually.

'Yes. Of course. But it isn't a suitable way to conduct yourself, Miss Sands,' she replied, just barely on the polite side of anger.

The Branch had disintegrated. Edna and Graham came less and less, then they married and stopped coming altogether. David was too busy working in the adult party to have time to turn up. A few years later there was a big photograph of him on the front page of the local paper during a bus-strike. It said 'Mr David Kent, the spokesman for the T&GWU'. So he must have changed his job and changed his union. Rick had a breakdown in his first year at Oxford. I bumped into him on a march, looking very pink and hurt. He said his girlfriend had left him – not Britt, it was another one by this time. Peter I imagined leading a charmed life in a charmed city, walking its streets with every right to be there; gliding in a boat between trees; sitting in lectures, hearing all there is to know, part of a beautiful idleness that should be youth. Sometimes in the public library, when sun shone through bits of stained glass, or I had just rummaged from a book a sentence about Love which seemed specially true, I imagined how it might be for him. But it was a tiny unplaced fragment in my life, just a glimpse of how I supposed his life must be all the time.

Eventually Fiddle rode back from the Continent on his patched-up motorbike, and customers at the Dog & Bear watched as he and a long-haired girl dismounted, walked round to a recently fitted sidecar and unpacked three small children and a copy of Bakunin. 'You can't get it over here,' said an excited Fiddle, fingering the pages lovingly, 'but she's going to translate it for me.'

He never went back to the GPO; he got a job in the local quarry and stopped coming into town much, just to sell copies of the Cuban paper *Granma*. The last reported sighting of him, he was a Man of the Trees. 'A what?' shrieked Gaily, who still hadn't learned how to type. The Men of the Trees – one of the first environmental groups.

Giving up on the idea of a transfer to another exchange, I moved to Nottingham and started work at a temp. agency.

Gaily Smith got married. I was still temping in Nottingham, but came over for the wedding.

It was a couple of years since we had met, and I was wondering what had happened to everybody at the Exchange. Chris and Mavis met me in the Spotted Horse. They looked pretty good, Mavis had lost her fly-away appearance and now held a position in the Union. 'Pamela's in charge now – guess what – Sal's had this really big promotion, she's in London now, working full-time at union headquarters. Julie and I are Pamela's deputies ... Judy? Judy's gone to Germany with her husband – he's teaching Forces' children. And – you'll never believe this – Rita is an acting supervisor!'

'A supervisor – Rita!'

Rita with the marmalade bouffant, Rita who rang the Barracks on Saturdays – it didn't seem possible, yet matched the unlikelihood of marriage, and they were all married now, and Chris had a little girl.

'Val Pepper left – she's an air-stewardess now.'

'Gosh.'

'Susan left as well – nobody seems to know what happened to her' – Chris looked at Mavis, who shook her head.

'Ronni? Ronni's married a Dutchman.'

'You must have got that wrong – don't you mean an Italian?' I said.

Chris looked upwards and then said patiently, 'No, fruit.'

'He was *foreign*,' I agreed, in the tone of one attempting to effect a compromise.

'Yes, he was foreign, he was Dutch,' said Chris, quite crossly for her.

'But I thought she wanted to marry an Italian,' I said, totally at sea.

'Well, I don't know anything about that, but Wendy had a lettercard from her, postmarked Amsterdam, with From Veronica van Gelderen written on the outside.'

Well, there you are – that's people for you. She went all the way round Italy and then she came back and married a Dutchman.

We all fell easily into the way of addressing each other as fruit, from long custom, although it was no longer in use in any of our current lives. We had another drink, and then put confetti in our bags and set off for the Council House, where the Registry Office was situated.

We turned into the Cornmarket and I fell behind.

'Come on,' called Chris.

'I'll catch you up,' I called back. I stood on the corner and watched them fleeting away towards the wedding. In a few minutes, Gaily with her new husband would come down the Council House steps in her mini and white boots with her flowers at one with the lilies in the old photograph of the first Retiring Room, blooming and then gone.

I walked into the square, past the war memorial. Never really noticed for years, a mother and baby, slightly raised yet intimate with shoppers and queuers for buses. As a child it had disturbed me, for she looked wounded, her stylised drapery I had taken for head-bandages. As my mother and I had waited for our bus I looked and couldn't understand, was never quite sure if they weren't both already dead. The lady with bent head held her baby so close to her face, tenderly, yet when you looked closely her face was granite. The wriggling little baby with outstretched arms seemed wonderfully alive, yet a horrible doom of blood and sacrifice lay upon them, going back to grandfathers and great-grandfathers, and before them. There are stark war memorials, and pretty ones with angels. But when you have angels Sacrifice is a word you can tint with gilt. This was a real mother, but when you looked for her face there was shadow.

The town clock chimed in the little market square, with its rattle of buses coming and going, its banks and shops and coffee-houses, the war memorial and the Guildhall with a poster showing Miss Blair's drama group in *Murder at the Vicarage*. More urgent messages – Sue waited til 8; Kenny ring me – were superseding the CND symbol put there by Rick and me, with our midnight paintbrushes.

Richard and Peter never came back. I used sometimes to wonder how they were. One time I saw Peter. I was leaning out of a train window, having been on an anti-Vietnam War demo. 'Is

215

that guy calling you?' said a girl I didn't know who was standing next to me. I looked in the direction she pointed and there, in the flapping shelter of CAMBRIDGE AGAINST THE WAR was Peter, shouting my name and waving with both arms enthusiastically. The train had begun to move but I didn't care, feverishly pulled at the stiff door-handle and started to get off. But then I saw there was a girl at his side and he bent and said something to her and she started to wave too. After the first dark heartbeat of disappointment I waved back, slowly. Everybody shouted and waved, the whole teeming station infectiously happy, situate in a benign and imperfect but improvable universe. All around the cries and wavings sounded ecstatic and deliriously expectant, as though our wanting it was keeping the world turning. I waved back, to him – to him mostly – to her, to everybody out there, to all of them in this bright day, as the train slowly gathered momentum, picked up speed and raced out of the 1960s.

A NOTE ON THE AUTHOR

Switchboard Operators is Carol Lake's
second collection of stories.